The Island

Mary Davis

Heartsong Presents

SEP 0 4 2007 KmA

To the Lord Jesus Christ for always being at my side.

To Mom, hoping one day you can visit Mackinac Island.

And to the men and women who spend their summers to make Mackinac Island a wonderful and unique experience for us all.

A note from the Author:
I love to hear from my readers! You may correspond with me by writing:

Mary Davis
Author Relations
PO Box 719
Uhrichsville, OH 44683

ISBN 1-59310-785-4

THE ISLAND

Copyright © 2005 by Mary Davis. All rights reserved. Except for use in any review, the reproduction or utilization of this work in whole or in part in any form by any electronic, mechanical, or other means, now known or hereafter invented, is forbidden without the permission of Heartsong Presents, an imprint of Barbour Publishing, Inc., PO Box 719, Uhrichsville, Ohio 44683.

All scripture quotations, unless otherwise indicated, are taken from the HOLY BIBLE, NEW INTERNATIONAL VERSION®. NIV®. Copyright © 1973, 1978, 1984 by International Bible Society. Used by permission of Zondervan Publishing House. All rights reserved.

All of the characters and events in this book are fictitious. Any resemblance to actual persons, living or dead, or to actual events is purely coincidental.

Our mission is to publish and distribute inspirational products offering exceptional value and biblical encouragement to the masses.

Cover design by Jocelyne Bouchard

PRINTED IN THE U.S.A.

one

Haley Tindale sucked in a quick breath through clenched teeth and pushed her shoulder into the hackney horse's shoulder until he removed his hoof from her foot. She let out her breath and wiggled her toes; nothing seemed broken.

Thunder blinked his big brown eyes at her as if knowing he'd done something wrong.

She stroked his nose. "I know you didn't mean it."

Horses weren't like people; they didn't intentionally hurt a person. Her bruised foot would heal with far less difficulty than her heart had from betrayal. She still wasn't ready to deal with that whole mess. And fortunately she wouldn't have to for at least six more weeks. It was amazing how free and uninhibited she felt away from her family. No expectations. No pressure. So until she left Mackinac Island in mid October, she would enjoy her time here and not think about her other life off the island.

Harry, the stable master, stepped around from behind her. "Over there. Sit. Take off your boot."

"What?"

He pointed to a wooden barrel set against the wall. "I saw what happened. I need to check that foot."

"It's fine, really. I've been stepped on by horses before. I know what a broken bone feels like."

Harry just stared at her from under his bushy brown eyebrows. He was a large, stocky fellow in his fifties.

She sighed as she sat, then tugged up the pant leg of her jeans and unlaced her work boot. Her foot smarted when she pulled off her boot. "He didn't even put his full weight on it." Thunder hadn't meant to do it. Not like Kennith, who knew exactly what he had been doing.

"The sock, too."

She complied.

Harry checked the bones on the top of her foot with a gentle touch that contrasted with his beefy hands. "Nothing broken, but you'll probably have a doozy of a bruise. You want the morning off to ice it?"

She shook her head and pulled on her sock. "I'll be fine. What do I do all day? Sit on a carriage seat. I can prop up my foot on the front edge of the carriage if I need to."

"Let me know if it gives you any trouble."

"I will." She tried not to show the pain of replacing her boot. This would heal in no time. She didn't need or want people fussing over her. She just wanted to do her job in a place where she was nothing special and no one cared to use her.

After double-knotting her boot, she went over and stroked Thunder's nose again. "I'd take you stepping on my foot over certain people any day." She pulled an apple and her pocketknife out of her jacket. She cut the apple down the middle, holding half in each flattened hand, one for Thunder and the other for his pulling mate for the day, Thor.

"You're going to spoil those horses," Harry called from the tack room.

She smiled. Nothing got by Harry. Besides, the horses were worth spoiling.

❧

Brent Walker stood at the bow on the top level of the passenger ferry with the wind blowing hard in his face. Maybe the wind would cleanse him of his apprehensions. He drank in deeply of the northern Michigan air. He still didn't like this case.

He'd become a private investigator because he thought he might like the job, but he didn't. Sooner or later in his life, he had to find something that fit. He couldn't keep drifting from one job to another, could he?

He'd asked the Lord to give him a case right away, and the Lord had been faithful. But as soon as he had agreed to take it and received the retainer, he saw a side of Mr. Jackson he didn't like—pushy and self-serving. He would have given the money back if not for the sad, helpless look on the face of the man's daughter. Something inside him wanted to help the young, pregnant Kristeen Jackson, so he hadn't returned the money. But he knew one thing: This would be his first and last case—searching far and wide for someone was not his gig. And working for a person like Mr. Jackson was not what he wanted to do ever again.

He watched Mackinac Island grow larger as the ferry raced toward it. The island sat between the upper and lower peninsulas of Michigan on the Lake Huron side of the Straits of Mackinac. He didn't know much about Mackinac, only that it was a popular vacation spot famous for the Grand Hotel—which he could see even now, white stretched against the green background—and that motor vehicles weren't allowed—just horses and bicycles. This ought to be interesting. It sounded like a place a person could hide if he wanted to.

He pulled out the picture of the blond-haired, blue-eyed youth and shook his head. How was he supposed to find this Justin Mikkelson, working on a vacation island during the height of tourist season, if he couldn't show his picture around or ask about him? Not only was the task like looking for a needle in a haystack, but he was expected to do so blindfolded.

Mr. Jackson had told him implicitly not to show the picture or ask about the boy. His reasoning? He said the minute this kid knew someone was looking for him, he would run again. So that was the requirement of the job—find Justin on sight alone. Did Mr. Jackson know how ridiculous his request was? If he did find Justin this way, nothing would stop him from running anyway. Brent had no authority to hold the boy or take him back. But maybe he could talk to him and get him to cooperate.

He shook his head and returned the small copy of the picture to his pocket. His best friend, Dalton, said it was going to be like bobbing for apples in Lake Michigan. This was definitely his last case.

❧

"Whoa." Haley pulled back on the worn leather reins in her hands. Thor and Thunder stopped where the next group of fudgies waited to board her twenty-passenger tour carriage. Thor shook his head, causing the traces to jingle.

Most tourists didn't even know the locals here on Mackinac Island, and those who worked the summer season referred to tourists as fudgies. With the thousands of pounds of island fudge bought and consumed each summer, how could they not have earned the name by association?

She took tickets, and several groups of passengers piled on board. She waited until they settled, then counted heads. Seventeen. Two vacancies toward the back and one up front. "I have room for three more."

The man at the front of the line said, "We have five."

She looked past the first five to the next in line, an older couple in their late sixties, she would guess.

"There are just two of us." The man stepped forward and handed her a pair of tickets. Then they climbed into the next to the last row.

It looked as if it would be a group of only nineteen this time, but she announced anyway, "I have room for one more." She scanned the line. Behind the next group of four, a ruggedly handsome man who looked to be in his early thirties, wearing khaki walking shorts and a five o'clock shadow, stepped forward with his index finger raised. She looked at the people near him, but no one seemed to be telling him they would catch up with him later. His brown hair was bleached on the ends and tousled on top.

He climbed into the seat behind her and flashed his ticket. Interesting. She couldn't recall ever having someone ride by himself. Everyone traveled in pairs and groups.

She took down her microphone and pressed the button as she turned in her seat. "Welcome aboard. I'm Haley. We'll travel up Main Street, past the Grand Hotel, and up to Surrey Hills for the middle part of the tour." She hung up her microphone, waited for a horse-drawn freight wagon to pass, then gave a click with her tongue and a small snap of the reins. Thor and Thunder heaved the carriage forward among the bicycle and foot traffic. On the island, horses had the right-of-way. Pedestrians and bicyclists, beware.

Her foot was aching where Thunder had stepped on it earlier that morning, so she propped it up on the front edge of the carriage. She maneuvered down Main Street and turned on Mahoney Avenue. She reached for her microphone and caught a glimpse of the last man to board, the Lone Ranger. He had a strong jawline and eyes that searched like a hawk after its prey. She pressed the button on her mike. "There are hundreds of lilac bushes on the island. The middle of June, when all the lilacs are in bloom, is the only time when you don't smell the road apples."

The older woman in the front seat asked, "What are road apples?"

Right on cue. Someone usually asked. If no one did, she let them draw their own conclusions. "Someone wants to know what road apples are. If you look out on the left"—she pointed to some horse droppings as they passed—"those are road apples." A few chuckles rippled through the carriage. They did give Mackinac a unique pungent aroma, but it was better than car exhaust.

As they headed up Cadotte Avenue, Thor settled into a lazy walk while Thunder heaved the full weight of the carriage. "Thor, gid-up." She tapped his hind end with her buggy whip. He twitched his ears and tail and grunted at her for being caught, but he picked up his share of the weight.

"The redbrick building on the left is the public school where the children of the five hundred year-round residents attend a K–12 program. On the right is the Little Stone Church. If you look up on the hill, you can see the governor's summer home. When the Michigan state flag is being flown, as it is today, the governor is in residence. The grassy area to the left of the stone church is the Grand Hotel golf course. And on the left are some of the grounds of the Grand Hotel." At the small median where West Bluff Road branched off to the left, she pulled on the reins, causing Thor and Thunder to come to a stop.

"The Grand Hotel was built in 1887. It was started in April after the spring thaw and was completed three months later.

The hotel opened on July 10. It seems amazing to build such a large structure in so short a time. But earlier this summer, I had a group of Amish riding in my carriage. One of them said, 'Well, I wouldn't think so. If we can put up a barn in a day, it shouldn't be any trouble to build a hotel in three months.'"

She hung up the microphone and stole another glimpse at the Lone Ranger in khaki shorts. He quickly diverted his gaze and brought his camera up to his face. Had he been watching her, rather than looking at the hotel?

She put her team into motion. *Well, of course, Haley, everyone was looking at you. You were the one talking. Duh.*

She tapped Thor's rump with the buggy whip. "Gid-up, Thor."

"Why do you keep telling Thor to giddy up?" someone in the second row asked.

She turned in her seat to answer without the mike and caught the Lone Ranger's gaze skipping to the passing scenery. "Thor gets lazy and lets Thunder do all the work, especially when they're pulling uphill. He thinks I don't notice and he can get away with it, while poor Thunder is huffing and puffing away. It's much easier to walk than to pull."

The Lone Ranger snapped a picture, of what, she wasn't sure. *The trees?* He rested the camera in his lap.

Why was he alone? It wasn't as if he had a third eye in the middle of his forehead or snarled at people. Despite his serious demeanor, he was pleasant to look at. He looked more like a man on a mission than a man on vacation. Tense. Didn't he know vacations were supposed to be fun and relaxing? Even though she was working, she was more relaxed and stress free than she had been in years. She had no big responsibilities, no one needing something from her, and no family pulling her in five directions wanting something—no one using her. She was free here.

She pulled her team to a halt. She had passed up one site and was about to pass up another. Distracted by a handsome stranger, just like a schoolgirl. She spoke into her mike and pointed out the two sites, then continued.

"We're approaching Surrey Hills. A museum and working blacksmith shop are there. Also gift and snack shops. At the far end of the building, you can catch the thirty-five-passenger carriage for the middle part of the tour. It will take you past the post cemetery, Arch Rock, the skull cave, and the fort." She pulled her team to a halt in front of the buildings. "You can also visit the Wings of Mackinac butterfly conservatory. You are welcome to stay as long as you like and catch the next available carriage. Have a good time, and enjoy your visit."

The Lone Ranger was the first to jump down; then he offered a helping hand to the two women in the front. She took a deep breath and watched as he disappeared inside the building. Since she rarely saw a fudgie more than once, that was probably the last she'd see of him. She talked a moment with the older couple who had boarded just before he did. They thanked her for a pleasant tour. If they only knew how off she was this trip. Then, after a glance toward the building, she clicked her team into motion and headed to the pickup spot.

❧

Brent Walker looked out the Surrey Hills gift shop window at the carriage driver who had just dropped them off. Haley, she had said her name was. She was speaking with an older couple who had been on the carriage and was smiling at them.

He raised his Nikon and pulled Haley into focus. Her hair was drawn back and twisted into one of those claw things that looked like a lethal weapon. The ends of her hair sprayed out the top of it like a happy fountain. What color did they call that? He'd had a girlfriend once with hair about that color who insisted it was blond, dishwater blond. He zoomed in on her face. Her warm and inviting smile tugged at him. He zoomed tighter on her smiling eyes. Not a hint of makeup. He backed off, and her wholesome face filled his lens. *Click.* Saved forever. As he tucked his camera back into his bag, he watched her pull away.

Brent had allowed himself to be distracted long enough. Time to get back to work. He toured the gift shop, museum, and blacksmith shop, snapping shots of any male who looked remotely as if he could pass for eighteen.

He boarded the larger carriage and took the second part of the tour. Nothing very interesting—and no Justin Mikkelson hiding from his short past. He got off at Fort Mackinac.

He paid his entrance fee. A battle was in progress between what looked like the Americans and the British. He scanned the soldiers with his telephoto lens and snapped several pictures. Numerous young men stood among the lesser ranks, and almost any one of them could be Justin Mikkelson shadowed behind a soldier cap. Justin had been in drama and performed a leading role in his senior play. Playing war could be right up his alley.

While the war ensued, Brent strolled through the fort exhibits, scanning for other young actors. No Justin. He exited to the central war zone as the Americans defeated the British. All was well, and history had not been changed in the last half hour.

He mingled among the soldiers and other actors. No baby-faced, blond-haired, blue-eyed Justin Mikkelson. *Where to now?* He rubbed the scratchy stubble on his face. Even when he had just shaved, it seemed as if he could use a shave. Winter couldn't come soon enough so he could forgo shaving altogether.

He should head out to catch the next carriage. He couldn't accomplish anything more here. He could always trek down the hill, but he would get enough exercise today traipsing up and down the streets and in and out of every shop. Shopping was a necessary evil unless it was at a music or electronics store. He wished he had a female friend along to send into the shops. Then again she could get distracted with all the paraphernalia and not accomplish anything for him. He could walk through all the shops in, let's say, an hour, then move on to the marina.

He slung his camera bag over his shoulder and headed to the loading area. Soon a carriage pulled up, but Haley was not at the reins. It was one of the larger carriages with three horses. Maybe he could catch her back at Surrey Hills. If he found Justin, he could come back for fun and maybe see Haley again. He hopped aboard and got off at Surrey Hills again. A carriage was pulling up, but no Haley. He buzzed through the butterfly conservatory, but Justin didn't work there. He stood outside with a small group of tourists. The next departing carriage filled fast, but his special seat behind the beautiful Haley was waiting for him. He flashed his ticket and climbed aboard.

Haley drove the carriage down past the Grand Hotel and turned on what she called Market Street. She pointed out several historical buildings, any one of which Justin could work in.

The microphone clicked, and Haley spoke again. "At the end of Market Street, on the left, is the Beaumont Memorial, a building named for Dr. William Beaumont, an army physician. On June 6, 1822, twenty-eight-year-old Alexis St. Martin, a French-Canadian voyageur, was accidentally shot in the stomach. Dr. Beaumont decided that since the boy wasn't likely to live, he would perform a harmless experiment on him. He tied small pieces of food to a string and put them in the hole in Alexis St. Martin's stomach. Dr. Beaumont's studies furthered scientific understanding of how the digestive system works. The boy outlived Dr. Beaumont by twenty-seven years." She maneuvered the horses through two consecutive right turns; then she wished them all a pleasant stay on the island.

It's over already? Brent reluctantly stepped down from the carriage and watched Haley drive up to collect her next group. He walked past the line of tourists waiting to climb aboard her carriage and gave her a quick salute as he passed. She gave him a nod. He stepped into the doorway of a shop two doors down and turned. He focused his camera on Haley and snapped a picture. She turned to her left and spoke to someone in the street. He pulled back the zoom to include the recipient of her attention. A blond male in good shape on a bicycle, who could easily be in his late teens, from what little he could see. The boy had his arm raised in front of his face to shade his eyes. He could be anyone. He snapped a picture anyway but kept the boy in his view. Brent zoomed in, hoping to get a glimpse of his face. But the boy dipped his head, turned his bike around, and pedaled off.

Brent snapped several pictures in succession, hoping one had caught the boy's face, then walked quickly, traversing the crowd in the direction he had gone. By the time he reached the corner, the boy was too far down the street to catch. Was it Justin?

two

Haley left the barn and straddled her bicycle. The rumble from her stomach bounced around inside her rib cage. She peddled to the Victorian Tea Shoppe on Market Street and waved to Veronique.

Her friend waved back and exited the shop a few moments later. Veronique's brown hair was blunt cut just below her jaw line, giving length to her round face. "I only have thirty minutes. Madame Oaks is not feeling well and wishes for me to—how do you say?—lock up zee doors."

"Close up." Haley loved listening to Veronique's heavy French accent. She spoke very good English with few problems. "Shane and Jason are supposed to have a table already." Once a week the four friends liked to treat themselves to dinner anywhere but the dining hall, trying different restaurants. Tonight it was the Yankee Rebel, one of their favorites. She could feel the bruise on her foot as she walked her bike, but the pain wasn't bad. Likely her foot would ache the more she was on it.

Jason stood on the sidewalk, and when he saw them, he waved to get their attention. The lowering sun turned his blond hair golden. His smile broadened as they drew closer, and his gaze settled on Haley.

She tried to ignore his attention. "Is Shane here?"

"He has a table in the back." He stepped to the doorway and motioned them inside. "After you, ladies."

Haley followed Veronique through the dimly lit rustic restaurant.

Shane stood up from a table in the back corner to be seen. "I ordered root beers all around." His blond hair looked brown in the low light.

Veronique smiled at Shane. "You know my weakness." She sat and took a long drink.

Jason pointed to Haley's chair and waited for her to sit. Then Jason and Shane sat. Jason had not been so polite at first but had learned quickly from Shane's almost natural manners. She had to make sure she treated them both equally and didn't encourage Jason's attention toward her.

They ordered, and then Veronique said, "Fudgie stories."

Veronique loved to hear and tell of the unique tourists. She wanted to take as many stories as possible back to her family in France. She was a glutton for any story.

"I will start." Veronique took a quick drink of her root beer. "Zese five women come in all dressed in violet shirts and trousers and wearing different kinds of big red hats. Some have flowers. Some have feathers. One wore a hat with a violet little bear with a red hat on. And zay said zay are some kind of hat group."

"The Red Hat Society." Haley's grandma was a member of a group in her hometown.

Veronique pointed at her. "Yes. Red Hat Society. Zat is what zay said. Zay were very sweet ladies and very funny. Zay buy anything with a red hat."

Since neither Jason nor Shane dealt with tourists, it was her turn. The first fudgie who came to mind was the rugged, maskless Lone Ranger. Her French friend, not being a driver, wouldn't likely understand the uniqueness of it. Or had it been his smile and that little salute-type wave after he had gotten off?

"So," Veronique prompted.

"I had a sweet older couple who were celebrating their fiftieth wedding anniversary. They were married on the island and spent their honeymoon here and came back fifty years later."

Veronique sighed. "Zat is so romantic. Zat is what I want to do, too."

Jason shot Shane a dubious look with a raised eyebrow, and Shane just shrugged. It didn't matter if they understood. Veronique was the one who wanted the story, and she did understand.

After they ate, Haley and Veronique went to the restroom. When they came out, Shane was waiting.

"Veronique, I'll walk you back to work."

Haley reached into her pocket for her money. "Let me pay, and I'll go, too."

Shane stopped her. "You haven't finished your chicken."

Veronique put her hand on Haley's arm. "Yes. Stay. I don't want to spoil everyone." Veronique headed through the restaurant for the door.

"Is Jason staying?"

Shane nodded. "He said he'd pay."

"I don't think that's a good idea."

Shane cocked his mouth up on one side. "He really likes you."

"That's why it's not a good idea. Come back after you walk Veronique to work."

"Jason asked me not to." Shane shrugged. "I have to catch up to Veronique." He walked away.

She squinted her eyes after him. *Mutineer.*

She went back to the table and quickly finished her meal. It didn't taste as good as it had before. The waiter brought the bill, and Haley put her hand over it.

Jason reached for it at the same time, and his hand covered hers. "I'll get it."

That would set a bad precedent between them. "My treat." She slipped her hand and the bill out from under Jason's hand, as he was starting to curl his fingers around hers.

She reached into the front pocket of her jeans and pulled out her cash. She hadn't planned to pay for everyone's meal and didn't have enough. She could use the credit card she normally carried just in case, but credit cards could be tracked. And she had done so well not using it so far. "Do you have a ten? I'm a little short."

Jason snatched the bill and paid it with his card.

Haley cringed inside.

"Do you want to walk around town?"

She gave him a weak smile as they left the Yankee Rebel. "One of the horses tromped on my foot this morning. I need to rest it." It was aching even now. "Besides, I'm beat. I'm going to hit my pillow and hope I wake to my alarm at oh-dark-thirty in the morning."

They headed up the street toward Haley's dorm. She much preferred having Shane walk her home. He didn't have any interest in her except friendship. Shane was like the brother she didn't have. And Jason, well, Jason wasn't content with only friendship. He was always trying to mold it into something more.

Jason broke the awkward silence. "So the summer's almost over. How about if we catch dinner together tomorrow night? Just the two of us, maybe at the Grand Hotel dining room?"

Why couldn't he take her first no as a permanent no? Why did he make her reject him over and over? "Jason, when did you graduate from high school?"

"In June. I'm a college man now." He held his hands out to his sides as some sort of proof. "I know you're a year or two older than me, but I don't care. I don't have any hang-ups about a girl being a little older."

"Try seven."

"Whoa." His jaw came unhinged. "That would make you like—like twenty-five. No way."

"Yes way. I graduated from college three years ago with a degree in futility." Music had been far from her father's choice of majors for her, and that was why she had chosen it—to show him she wasn't his puppet. But Daddy ignored her major and somehow roped her into the family business anyway. She still wasn't sure how it happened. Grandpa being ill had played a part, but there was more she couldn't put her finger on. She had changed all that, however. Mackinac was far from Daddy and the rest of her manipulative family.

"Seven years. That's not so much. I could live with it."

She sighed silently. Jason, like Daddy, didn't seem to understand the word *no*. "Jason, I just don't think it would work between us."

"You don't know until you try." He flashed his irresistible grin.

But she could resist. "As you said, summer's almost over—no good starting something now."

"It could be good. We could create some serious sparks."

She locked her bike for the night and stopped at the door to her dorm. "Thank you for walking me home, Jason." She hoped he would take it for the dismissal it was.

"I'm not giving up yet." He winked and headed across the street.

She took a deep breath and watched him go. *Lord, please change his heart and make him finally give up or focus on heading to Western Michigan U or anything but me.*

❧

Brent connected the USB cable from his camera to his laptop sitting on the table. He turned on the computer, and soon the pictures were downloading. He listened to Dalton beating the drums in the garage. He recognized the harshness to the strikes. He'd go out and jam with him with his electric guitar if his friend weren't so set on abusing his drum set. Dalton still hadn't healed from his wife's death three years ago.

Brent's longtime friend had welcomed his visit. Dalton's two-bedroom house on the mainland in Mackinaw City faced the bridge but was a couple of blocks from the water.

He enlarged each photo to the size of the screen and studied every face in the crowd. Then suddenly Haley, the friendly carriage tour driver, filled his screen. He sat back in the chair and smiled at her. He studied the way the light shone on the apples of her cheeks and the squint of her smiling eyes. Her hair had to be fairly long for the size weapon holding it back. Then he noticed a small silver chain around her neck. The shot was too close to see what hung from it. He flipped through several dozen shots until he came to the ones he'd taken after he got off her carriage the second time. Her hand was holding whatever hung from the chain. But the edge barely peeked out. He highlighted the area and enlarged it but couldn't see what it was. He was about to enlarge it again when Dalton came through the garage door. He quickly clicked to the next picture and turned to his friend.

Dalton stopped in midstride. "When did you get back?"

"A little while ago."

"Want to go down the street and get something to drink?"

He shook his head. "I have a lot of pictures to go through before I hit the hay."

Dalton inclined his head toward the screen. "Who's that?"

He almost said Haley's name without looking but turned and was glad he hadn't. "Don't know." It was the kid who was talking to Haley he had tried to chase down.

"Is that the boy you're looking for?"

"Could be, but it's hard to tell. I couldn't get a clear shot of him. His basic build and coloring fit."

Dalton worked as a play actor, a captain in the American forces, at the original site of the fort on the Lower Peninsula before it was moved to Mackinac Island and the name shortened. "I asked around Fort Michilimackinac, but no one has heard of a Justin Mikkelson."

"Thanks."

"I'm going to make a sandwich. You want one?"

"I ate on the island."

As Dalton headed for the kitchen, Brent turned back to his computer. Was it the boy? He pulled out the small photo he'd copied from Kristeen's yearbook and held it up to the screen. Justin was smiling in the copy but not on the screen. In one, his hair looked lighter than the other, but lighting could do that. It could be. But then again, it could be anyone.

He stared longer and held the picture at different angles. Something about this boy made him want to pursue it. He couldn't rule him out. And if it was Justin, the informative Haley knew him and could be a huge asset in locating him.

three

The next day when Brent got off the ferry, he scanned the shops up one side of the street and down the other. He'd only stepped into a fraction of them yesterday before he thought he'd go crazy. He could not see how women shopped for fun. Just the thought was nauseating.

If that boy he'd seen yesterday by the carriage was Justin, then maybe if he hung out with that carriage driver for a while, he'd get a better glimpse of him and know one way or the other. And what were the chances that an eighteen-year-old boy would be working in one of the shops? That wouldn't have been his choice fourteen years ago.

Shops or another carriage ride? A compromise was in order. He could loop through the few stores between here and the ticket booth, then hop another carriage ride. If he only scoped out a handful of tourist traps at a time, maybe it wouldn't be so bad. After five places, he stared at how many still stood between him and the carriage-tour ticket booth. As he surveyed the next yawning edifice waiting to swallow him, he rubbed his mouth with his hand, his whiskers scratching his palm, then jogged across the street, dodging two cyclists.

As he approached the tour company, he noticed Haley sitting aboard the next departing carriage. She wore blue jeans and a white T-shirt with her hair pulled back in that claw thing, same as yesterday. He hustled to the ticket window and glanced back at Haley's carriage. "Are there still seats available on that carriage?"

"Yes, sir."

Thank You, Lord. "I'll take one." He snagged his ticket and went for the carriage. Would she remember him?

As he handed his ticket to Haley, her eyes widened slightly. "Welcome back."

She did recognize him. That was a positive sign. "Thank you." He gave her a slight nod and caught a glimpse of her silver necklace, a cross made out of nails. He had a larger version of it on a black leather cord that he'd bought after he'd rededicated his life to the Lord eleven years ago when he was twenty-one. A person wouldn't wear that style of cross unless he personally knew the Man who bore those nails for him. So chances were excellent that this lovely young tour guide was a Christian. That thought stretched his mouth into a smile. Where was his cross? In his shaving bag? He'd have to look for it.

The first seat was full, so he boarded in the second row. As the tour went from town up to Surrey Hills, he took a few pictures and let Haley's voice wash over him.

"Gid-up, Winston." Haley tapped the hind end of a caramel-colored horse with the buggy whip.

So today it was Winston slacking off. Was there always one horse in a pair that tried to get away with it? What would happen if both horses decided to let the other do the pulling? Not much.

As the first row of tourists disembarked at Surrey Hills, he stepped over the seat to the front, leaning forward, and caught Haley's scent of fresh hay and sunshine. Not that sunshine actually had a smell, but it was clean and warm. She had a piece of hay in her hair. Would she think it weird if he plucked it out? He sat and rested his forearms on his thighs. "I'm not interested in taking the other carriage around. May I just stay on?"

She turned to him with a smile. "People usually get off and look around. Then a line forms over there."

He jumped down and headed for the invisible line.

Haley guided her team forward, and as the carriage halted, he spread his arms. "No one here but me. Who would have thought that on the first tour of the day everyone would want to see the museum and the other loop of the tour?"

"I rarely have passengers on the first return run."

He stood straight and gave her a salute. "Permission to come aboard, ma'am?"

"I was going to tell you that you could stay on, but you jumped down too quickly." She waved him on. "So why no sightseeing today?"

He settled in. "I'm seeing plenty from your carriage. It's helping me decide where else to go."

"A tour guidebook would be cheaper."

"But not nearly as interesting." He draped his arms on the back of the seat. "And it can't answer questions."

She put both reins in her left hand and turned in her seat. "What kind of questions?"

"Like how many people work on the island in the summer?"

"I don't know." She rested her free hand on her thigh. "People from all over the world work here. So, hundreds, probably thousands."

"That many?"

"Between the shops, attractions, hotel staff, drivers, maintenance crews, stable hands, dockworkers, marina employees"—she sucked in a deep breath—"the actors at the fort. . .it goes on and on."

He was definitely looking for a needle. "Where do all those workers live?"

"Some in dormitories; a lot live above the many shops. Some local residents rent out rooms in their houses."

The horses stepped forward, and she turned to the front, pulling on the reins. "Whoa, boys." She turned back to him. "They think it's time to leave."

He nodded. "So who feeds all those people?"

"The tour company has a dining hall. Other large island employers feed their own. And for a fee, some of the dining halls will let you buy a meal ticket."

"So do you know a lot of the people who work on the island?"

She readjusted the reins in her hands. "I guess I know quite a few. Why all the interest? Are you planning to apply for a job next summer?"

It couldn't be any worse than any of the other things he'd tried. And certainly no worse than his current job. "No, I was just curious. What do you all do in your off time?"

"I sleep or read. But some have favorite hangouts."

"Yesterday someone asked about churches. Are the workers able to go to church?" That might narrow down this haystack.

"A couple of the churches on the island offer a six a.m. service for those of us who have to work on Sundays. I also help lead a Bible study on Tuesday nights."

Justin's aunt, whom he lived with, said Justin was a strong Christian, so he would probably go to early church and a Bible study. Though he wasn't supposed to ask, he didn't see how it could hurt if he veiled it. "I met a woman who said her nephew was working on Mackinac Island. Maybe you know him. Justin Mikkelson?"

She shook her head. "I don't know any Justins here."

He watched her body language: no dilating pupils, no

fidgeting, no reddening of the ears, none of the telltale signs of lying. "Maybe he goes by his initials or a middle name. Any Mikkelsons? I'd really like to tell him hello from his aunt."

"Sorry. I know a Jason Mitchel. But no Mikkelson."

Was that a dead end or simply a detour? Maybe he could come at it from a different angle. "So why do people come from all over the world to work on this island?"

"Lots of reasons."

That was too general of an answer to be any help. But it was an interesting question, and though it had nothing to do with finding Justin, he was curious to know Haley's reason. "Why did *you* come to Mackinac Island to work?"

"I ran away from home."

Just like that. No compunction, no hesitation, no explanation. Did she run away from a husband-and-child family or parents? "Aren't you a little old to be a runaway?" This island seemed to be a refuge for people who wanted to hide.

"With a family like mine, it was long overdue."

"Bossy and overbearing?"

She hesitated. "I think I've said enough about me."

"Come on. You can't make a comment like that and not tell me more. I would really like to know what kind of family would cause you to run away."

She squinted and moved her mouth back and forth, contemplating him.

"Please."

Her expression opened up again, and her shoulders relaxed. "Users. Everyone needed something from Haley. Dad, to get back in Grandpa's good graces. Grandpa doesn't like anyone in the family except me for some reason. But since running away, I'm probably on his this-no-good-family list, too. Mom, to keep the house running smoothly so she could look good volunteering at every charitable event that came her way. I've bailed my sister out of jail three times with the promise not to tell Dad and Mom. And. . ."

He waited a moment. "And what? Or should I say who?"

The tops of her ears reddened. "And the dog would hide under my bed when he was in trouble for chewing Dad's shoes beyond recognition."

He sensed a change in subject. "Was that the straw?"

"Straw?"

"The last straw—the reason you left home?"

She gave him a look that told him she didn't want to admit any more to a stranger. "It all adds up. I got tired of being surrounded by irresponsible people."

"And one day, you packed your bags and left for no apparent reason."

She looked toward a shop employee who strode toward her carriage. When she made eye contact with him, he said, "No takers. You can head out."

She waved an acknowledgment, then turned back to Brent. "Last chance to get off."

He leaned back and stretched out his legs. He might as well enjoy his solo trip with Haley. For some reason, he still had a feeling Haley knew Justin Mikkelson, but he was equally convinced she didn't know it. Was Justin using an alias? Jason Mitchel perhaps? Both did have the same initials. That seemed a little too obvious.

Haley turned in her seat. "Since you've taken the tour before, do you just want to be driven into town or do you want the spiel?"

He pushed thoughts of Justin from his mind. "What I'd

really like is to know more about you."

"I think I've told you enough about me."

"What time do you get off?"

"If you're asking me out, the answer is no. I don't date fudgies."

Perceptive. And she wasn't into playing games. No feigned surprise that he was trying to ask her out. Straight and up front. He liked that. Unless she was playing hard to get. He shook that thought away. She didn't seem the type. "What would a *fudgie* be?"

She pulled her mouth back in a grimace. "Sorry. I meant to say tourist."

"So people who work here call tourists 'fudgies'? Why is that?"

She lifted her shoulder. "Tourists buy thousands of pounds of fudge each summer, hence the affectionate nickname."

"But what if I haven't bought any fudge?"

"Guilt by association."

He snapped his fingers. "What if I quickly got a job here—then would you go out with me?"

She chuckled.

"I know the problem. You don't know enough about me. I'm devoted to the Lord and look forward to seeing Him in heaven one day. I became an emancipated minor at sixteen after my dad died. I have a great truck with an awesome sound system. And I play electric guitar. I've been in the Peace Corps and gone on twelve mission trips with church groups. I'm an all-around great guy, but don't ask me to cook." He skipped the part about working at various jobs and not having a permanent home.

"I'm afraid I'm still going to have to say no."

"How do you do that?"

She raised her eyebrows. "Do what?"

"Turn a guy down but still make it sound like a gift."

"You are something else." She shook her head. "Do you always lay it on this thick?"

"It's all your fault. I look at you, and it just comes out."

Haley laughed. She had a pleasant, soothing laugh. And he was glad he'd said something to evoke it from her. It was worth the rejection.

She pulled back on the reins. "End of the line, bud."

He looked around surprised they were already back in town. "You have to eat sometime. Lunch?" He didn't know why he was even asking. To get her to smile again?

She did smile and shook her head. "Go see the island."

"Thanks for the ride." He jumped down and held up his camera. "May I take your picture? To remember my trip by." She nodded and smiled down at him. He clicked the shutter, then gave her a salute and headed for the closest open door. He looped through the shop—no Justin—then stood at the window. Haley was greeting her next group of passengers. Why was he drawn to her?

Lord? Are You trying to tell me something about her? Does she really know Justin but doesn't realize it? Should I stay close to her? Or is she just an attractive woman who has hit a sweet spot with me?

The longer he was around her, the longer he wanted to be around her. She pulled away for her next tour. He took a deep breath. Back to work.

four

Brent sat at Dalton's kitchen table with his laptop open. One by one, he moved the general pictures into a Mackinac Island folder. He only had a handful today and none he thought would be useful. Then he moved the handful of pictures of a particular carriage driver into a folder he labeled *Hailey*. He wondered how she spelled it. It was one of those names that could have as many variations as the people with that name, unlike his with exactly one spelling. No one ever misspelled Brent.

He enlarged the second picture to fit the screen. Haley sat in her driver's seat and smiled down at him as he had clicked the shutter. Haley, the adult runaway. Her voice played through his head.

I got tired of being surrounded by irresponsible people. Her words mixed with the worn-out recording of Michelle's. *"My dad thinks you're irresponsible."*

"Who cares what he thinks. What do you think?"

"I care for you deeply, Brent."

"But you think I'm irresponsible, too."

"I just want to know what to expect. I want stability."

Irresponsible people.

Irresponsible.

Irresponsible.

He closed his laptop and pushed back from the table. How did one define irresponsibility? How did Haley define it?

Brent stood and went through the door out to the weight room that had been converted from a garage and also housed Dalton's drum set and electronic keyboard. "Do you think I'm irresponsible?"

Dalton lay on his back on his weight machine, doing crunches on an incline bench. "How so?" He grunted before curling back down.

"In life, in work, in general."

Dalton curled up and hooked his arms around his knees. "In life? You were always there for me, especially when I needed you most."

Brent remembered how frail and withered Dalton's wife, Joslin, had looked at the end. And how distraught Dalton had been.

His friend continued. "In work? Have you ever been fired? Besides the time you were fifteen and we both got fired."

He shook his head. "But I've never kept a job for more than eleven months in my life."

"By choice?"

"I just haven't found anything that fits right."

"Do you always give two weeks' notice?"

He nodded again.

"Very responsible." Dalton shifted his position slightly. "You've had a job or jobs since you were fifteen; you support yourself and always give notice before leaving. Sounds responsible to me. So in general, I'd say you're a responsible kind of guy." He swung his legs off the bench and grabbed his towel. "What's this all about?"

"I was thinking about Michelle."

"Now that's your first problem. She was never your type."

"I was in love with her."

"Isn't she married now?"

"Yes. But that doesn't stop her words from haunting me. I've proposed to three different girls in my life. They all turned me down. Why? What's wrong with me?"

"You just haven't met the right pre–Mrs. Brent Walker. It'll happen."

He wouldn't mind finding out if Haley was a potential Mrs. Brent Walker. "So you don't think that because I live out of my truck I'm irresponsible?"

"You're a minimalist."

"The sound system in my truck is better than most people have in their homes."

"Hey. I've got a decent system."

"So you're saying there is absolutely nothing wrong with me?" Then why couldn't he find a life partner?

"Well, you could use a few cooking lessons." Dalton stood and wiped his face with the towel. "I didn't think anyone could ruin burgers on the grill. Those things were leather."

"It's a gift." Dalton should have known what he was getting into, asking a man who lives out of his truck to cook. Then Brent blurted out, "I have a trust fund."

His friend did a double take.

"And a bank account with a substantial amount in it from my mom's insurance policy."

Dalton lowered himself back down onto the incline bench and stared.

"I never told anyone."

"Why did you live so frugally, skimping, sometimes barely having enough to eat until your next paycheck? You were working two jobs to make ends meet after your dad's insurance money ran out. I thought you never had an apartment for very long because you couldn't afford it."

"When Dad died, he had a will. He left everything to me. That wasn't a big deal until the lawyer told me about the bank account with the insurance money from Mom. Dad left a letter. Said he couldn't bring himself to spend it. He would've rather had Mom back than any amount of money. After I was born, Mom insisted on life insurance for both of them. She wanted to be sure I was taken care of. It was the lawyer's idea for me to become emancipated at sixteen. He was afraid someone would take me in and spend my money."

"And the trust fund? Did your dad do that, too?"

He shook his head. "My grandparents."

"I didn't know you had any grandparents."

"They died before Mom did but set up the fund when I was born. They felt my dad was irresponsible"—*there was that word again*—"and didn't want him to have any of their money. And if they left it to my mom, Dad would have access to it, too."

"Wow." Dalton stared at him. "Why didn't you blow through it at sixteen?"

He shook his head slowly. "I couldn't touch any of the money in the trust until I was twenty-five. And it never seemed as if it were mine anyway. Like it was set aside for a special purpose, but I don't know what that is. I feel as if my grandparents must have had something in mind and wouldn't approve of my spending it on something else." So it sat in a bank growing—he supposed, waiting. For what, he didn't know.

❧

Haley sat cross-legged on the floor in the church. Bjorn was giving his input on the lesson. Bjorn and Astrid were a couple who came from Sweden to work on the island. They had quite a diverse group in the Bible study: four Canadians, two women from England, one from China, a Filipino, an Israeli, an Aussie, and, of course, Veronique from France. The Lone Ranger would probably fit nicely into this group. He'd said he was a Christian. Being in a Bible study with someone was a good way to gauge the depth of their faith, to see if their beliefs matched your own. Something she hadn't had with Kennith. A mistake she would never make again.

She focused back on Bjorn and realized he had stopped speaking and Jason had started in. Whereas Bjorn appeared to be honestly seeking to deepen his faith, Jason seemed to try to say the right things. His faith seemed taped onto the outside. Another good reason not to go out with him.

What would it be like to go out with the Lone Ranger? She shook her head. What was she thinking? She didn't date tourists, and she didn't date coworkers; that pretty much took care of the island. She had been asked out a time or two by a tourist, but none as persistent or as tempting as this one. But no matter how tempting, she was going to stand her ground. No fudgie dating!

Pay attention, Haley. Lord, I'm sorry for being so distracted. Help me stop thinking about that man.

Jason finished talking. *And, Lord, please deepen Jason's faith.*

She gave him a nod, then looked around the group. "Anyone else?" She closed her Bible and folded her hands. "Then let's close in prayer." She bowed her head and prayed for the international group, then added a silent one for her own ridiculous thoughts about a stranger she would never see again. The group quickly dispersed because they all had to get up before the sun to be ready for the next day's fudgie invasion. She walked in the dark with Veronique, Shane, and Jason.

They had an arrangement within the Bible study; whenever

any of the girls walked at night, one of the guys would go with them. And they could call for a walking partner any time of the night if they needed to. Though the island was relatively crime free, they operated on the better-safe-than-sorry policy.

As Haley walked beside Veronique, Shane and Jason walked behind them.

"Fudgie stories," Veronique said.

Jason and Shane both groaned.

Veronique ignored them and took her arm. "Who was your most interesting fudgie today?"

"The Lone Ranger." It was out before she thought.

"Who is zis Lone Ranger?"

She couldn't deny it now. "Just some guy who rode my carriage yesterday and today alone."

Jason and Shane moved up beside them, suddenly interested in the fudgie story.

"What is wrong with riding alone?" Veronique asked.

If she could only pull her words back. But it was too late. "Nothing. Most people come to the island with other people and ride the carriage together. I can't remember anyone riding by himself before."

"Did you report him?" Jason said.

She pulled her eyebrows together. "Why? He's done nothing wrong." She noticed Shane and Veronique giving Jason questioning looks, as well.

"He's by himself, and he's picked out your carriage two days in a row. That's intentional," Jason said, trying to defend his question.

Shane spoke up then. "I know the worst crime we have to worry about on the island is a 'borrowed' bike now and again, but be careful."

Jason jumped back in. "Yeah, be careful. This guy could be a stalker or something."

A stalker? She could not picture him as a stalker. She noticed Shane roll his eyes. "Well, you don't have to worry about that. I'll likely never see him again. It was probably just a fluke." What would Jason say if she told him this man had asked her out? She didn't want to know.

Later, after she'd gone to bed, she closed her eyes, picturing the Lone Ranger's face and pairing it with the word *stalker*. The two didn't seem to go together. *Lord, are my friends right? Should I be concerned about this guy? Is he a threat?* She thought of his smile and pictured him saying, "I'm devoted to the Lord and look forward to seeing Him in heaven one day." He hadn't said he was a Christian or that he believed in God, two things a lot of people would say. People who had a deeper belief might say something more like what he said. And it was the first thing out of his mouth about himself, not tacked on as an afterthought.

She wished she could erase his smiling face from her mind. But what was so bad about having a good-looking man plastered to the inside of her eyelids? He would be gone by morning. She sighed and rolled to her side. *Goodnight, Lone Ranger.*

five

Haley settled in for another day's work—though the word *work* did not describe how she felt about her job. She loved the tranquillity of the island, and she especially loved working with the horses. Today she had Golddust and Pete. Golddust was the one to watch today. Whenever he headed up toward Surrey Hills, he wanted to keep going to the barn. Every run was quitting time for him. He was due for time off after today's shift.

She pulled up to the curb to receive her first load of passengers. A smile pulled at her mouth when she saw the Lone Ranger climb aboard her carriage. "You're a glutton for punishment." She noticed he wore a cross made out of nails on a worn black cord similar to her own. Dressed much the same way as the previous two days: T-shirt, fleece jacket, walking shorts, and hiking boots.

He sat in the seat behind her, to her left. "I hear a carriage tour is a good way to see Mackinac Island." He smiled broadly in satisfaction.

"There are a variety of other ways to see the island that you haven't already seen on your other two carriage tours."

"Like?"

"Like bicycling around the island and then through the interior. You can rent a horse and ride almost anywhere. Or you could take a cruise around the island on a yacht. You would get a more well-rounded view of Mackinac instead of a single perspective."

He scratched his head with a goofy look on his face, pretending to think. "But what would I do with all these tickets?" He fanned out several tickets, all for the carriage tours.

"You bought that many tickets? You'll be riding all day."

"That's the idea. I'll be right in this seat the whole time."

"Why would you want to hear the same drivel all day long?"

"There's a pretty tour driver I'd like to get to know better. I figured if she wouldn't go out with me, then I'd go out with her. All day." He tapped his tickets against his palm, then tucked them back into the pocket of his navy fleece jacket.

That was bolder than she'd expected. She should say something back, but nothing came to mind. Since when did she have trouble shooting back a reply?

Be careful. He could be a stalker.

Stalker? She didn't think so last night. But that was when she thought she'd never see him again. Now he was back. All day. *Lord, was that a caution from You?*

I bore those nails for you and for him.

She fingered the cross hanging around her neck. This cross meant something to her. The Lord, her Lord, took those nails for her. Did it mean as much to him? She turned to see if she could read it in his face.

He smiled at her and wiggled his eyebrows. With her carriage full, she turned back, unclipped her mike, and spoke into it. "Welcome to Mackinac Island. I'm Haley. If you haven't bought fudge yet, Mackinac Island is famous for its fudge. You haven't truly experienced the island until you've experienced our fudge." Then she went on with her tour intro and set Golddust and Pete into motion.

She shouldn't have looked back. It only encouraged him. But he did seem sweet. Gorgeous didn't fit him. He was more a

Harrison Ford, Indiana Jones type of handsome, a little bit rough around the edges and seasoned to perfection. But none of that mattered because she was *not* going to date a fudgie. Even if he looked that good and was destined to be on her carriage all day.

She felt a tap on her shoulder and turned, staring straight into his endearing face. Her pulse quickened.

"Aren't you going to tell them that joke?"

She looked around and was startled that the horses had taken her farther than she realized. If she told the joke now, it would run into when she should talk about the next site. "I'll tell it later." She usually told the joke at one of two places. If a front-seat passenger was talkative, she saved it for the stretch just before Surrey Hills.

She had to get a grip. She wasn't some silly schoolgirl who melted at a handsome guy's feet. After she pointed out the sites, she decided she should tell the joke before her brain went fluffy on her again. "Here's a little island humor. What goes *clippity-clop, clippity-clop, clippity-clop, bang, clippity-clop-clop*?" She paused a moment to let her passengers think, then said, "A drive-by shooting on Mackinac Island."

Some laughed right away, others took a moment, and then a few wouldn't be able to find the humor in it even after it was explained. She hung up her mike.

"I love corny humor. And your timing is impeccable." The Lone Ranger had leaned way forward, right by her ear. There couldn't be much of him left on the seat.

Haley let out a slow breath between her pursed lips. The day was heating up earlier than usual. Was it going to be a scorcher?

Though a part of her wanted him to stay that close, she said, "Please remain seated." This was not the time or place to be developing a go-nowhere romance.

As the carriage neared the turnoff for Surrey Hills, Golddust picked up the pace, apparently hoping she would let him charge on by and quit for the day. Haley reined him in. Golddust swished his tail, slackened his stride, and followed Pete's lead.

❧

After several runs, Haley said to the Lone Ranger, "Time to get off."

"I still have more tickets." He dug the tickets out of his pocket as proof.

"If you want to use them, you'll have to hop on another carriage. These horses are finished for the day, and I'm going to lunch."

He jumped down. "Lunch? I'll buy."

She bit her top lip to help control her smile. "I have plans."

"When will you be back?"

"After lunch."

"What time is that?" He looked like a little boy begging to keep a stray puppy.

"When I get here."

He nodded and held up his tickets. "I'll see you this afternoon."

Maybe she would, and maybe she wouldn't. He could decide he'd had enough of the same old Mackinac Island sights and history. She headed to the barn and helped remove the harnesses and traces from Golddust and Pete. She was glad she'd brought a box lunch from the dining hall this morning. She did not look forward to Jason's interrogation when he asked if she'd seen the Lone Ranger today. She would have to tell him yes; then the questions and accusations would begin.

It was nice to have friends who cared about her safety, but she didn't feel it was necessary in this case.

After a quiet lunch, she retrieved her carriage with a fresh team of horses. She would spend the afternoon with Bruiser and Brutus, a pair of chestnut drafts, brothers. As she pulled her carriage to a halt behind the one loading, she saw the Lone Ranger leaning against a building, fiddling with his camera. His fleece jacket hung over his camera case. He'd actually waited for her.

He glanced up, and as he started to look back down, he jerked his gaze toward her and smiled. He put his camera into his shoulder bag and pushed off the wall. As he reached her carriage, so did John from the tour company ticket office.

John stepped aboard. "Big John wants to see you inside."

"I can't leave the horses. You know that."

"I'll hold them." John reached for the reins.

She set the safety break and handed the reins over before stepping down. The Lone Ranger nodded to her as she passed by. Once she was inside, Big John took her to his small office. Although he wasn't any bigger than the other John, they had to have some way of distinguishing the two, and Big John was the other John's superior. Big John was a willowy sort of fellow with a shock of thinning brown hair. "Jessica said a man bought enough tickets to ride all day and that he was in your carriage all morning."

She swallowed. "Yes." Why did she suddenly feel guilty? Because she was secretly enjoying harmless attention from a stranger?

"I'm concerned. Is he giving you any trouble? Should I have Morris check him out?"

Oh no, not the sheriff! She didn't want to get him in trouble.

"He hasn't been a problem. He mostly sits there and makes casual conversation like any of the other passengers. I don't think there is any reason to bother the sheriff."

"Are you sure?"

She wasn't absolutely sure, but he did seem harmless. "Yes."

"If he gives you any trouble at all, call in."

"I will. But I don't think that will be necessary." She had a feeling he was only a nice guy passing his time by flirting with her. She refused to read more into it than that.

She walked back to her carriage and relieved John of the reins.

With his back to where the Lone Ranger stood a few feet from the carriage, John gave her a wide-eyed look of concern.

"Thank you, John."

John walked away but didn't look too convinced, and the man stepped aboard. "Was that about me?"

She raised her eyebrows. "Why would you think that?"

"Call it a hunch. It seemed unexpected for you to be called away from your carriage. And your man John kept shooting glares at me the whole time you were gone."

"Oh." He didn't miss much.

"So?"

"So what?" She didn't want to explain that her friends thought he could be up to no good.

"Now you're going to start playing games?"

How to put it gently? "It's just unusual for someone to ride so much."

"I'm not a threat to you. I hope you know that."

"That's what I told him. I hope I'm right."

"You have my word. And if you tell me to get off and never ride your carriage again, I will."

She believed he'd do that.

"Haley, do you want me to get off?"

The earnestness of his voice touched her, and she really didn't want him to get off, so she could do nothing but be honest. "You can stay."

Her carriage filled, and she set the horses into motion. At the time for the drive-by shooting joke, she took down the mike.

The Lone Ranger leaned forward. "Can I tell it?"

She stared at him a moment, a little surprised. "Why not?" He took the mike and told the joke.

It sounded fresh the way he told it. It had gotten stale for her, telling it numerous times a day, week in and week out. The passengers laughed just the same. It was always fresh to them.

⁂

Haley was usually glad for the end of the day. The carriage seat made her stiff and sore, but today she wasn't so anxious for it to end. "The ride's over."

He jumped down but kept one hand on the carriage. "Have dinner with me?"

It was tempting. She wanted to say yes. *No fudgie dating.* Her declaration to herself rang in her ears. "I have plans."

"After dinner then." He didn't give up.

She shook her head. "I don't think so."

"I'll be in the park down the street between seven and nine. See you then." He winked at her.

Big John stepped onto her carriage. "I'll ride to the barn with you." Once they got under way, he said, "You're meeting him later?"

"I never said that. He's going to be in the park and wants me to meet him there after dinner."

"I hope you're not planning to. I don't think it's a good idea."

She hadn't planned on anything at this point. But she had to admit that a part of her wanted to meet him.

"What's his name?" Big John asked.

"I have no idea."

He turned to her. "You didn't get his name?"

She looked at him as Brutus and Bruiser gladly pulled the carriage up the hill toward home. "Should I have? I don't think I've ever asked a fudgie their name."

"No, I guess not. It would be nice to know in the event he. . .decides to cause any trouble."

Trouble? He was more likely to take over her job and tell corny jokes than cause trouble.

❧

Haley scooted toward Veronique to make room at the table for Jason and Shane. She turned her tray sideways to accommodate theirs at the table for eight that now sat nine. Shane tried to take the seat next to her, but Jason won it.

"So did the 'Lone Ranger' show up today?" Jason tried to sound casual, but Haley could hear the accusation in his question.

She swallowed hard on her half-chewed lasagna. Should she try to evade his questions or end the torture and tell him everything? "Yes." Maybe he would be satisfied with a simple answer to a simple question.

Jason turned in his chair. "Did he ride in your carriage or talk to you?" Accusations again.

"As a matter of fact, he did both."

"We have to tell someone," Jason said emphatically. "He could be dangerous."

She took a deep breath. "He's no more dangerous than you or Shane."

"How do you know?"

She could tell him it was none of his business, but that would imply she was trying to hide something. And she wasn't. "Because I spent all day with him."

"You what?" Jason said, with Shane echoing him a half beat behind.

"He bought enough tickets to ride all day." She might as well tell them the rest and be done with it. She had nothing to hide. She told them about the whole day, including being asked to lunch and dinner and meeting him in the park.

"You're not going." Jason's stern voice carried to the nearby tables. He didn't even try to intone it like a question.

What was it about someone telling her she couldn't do something that made it all the more appealing? "Big John would like to know what his name is." She wouldn't mind knowing either.

"Then let Big John meet him."

"I think it is romantic."

Jason glared at Veronique. "You would. You're French."

"What is zat supposed to mean?" If Veronique had been standing, Haley was sure her hands would have been on her hips. "Men! No. Boys!" Veronique turned to her. "Zay know nothing. Follow your heart."

"Tell me you aren't going," Jason demanded.

"I told him I wouldn't be there. Now can we drop it?"

Jason huffed and stabbed at his lasagna. She dared a glance at Shane. He looked disappointed in her, as if he knew she'd go, then turned back to his food. Well, it couldn't hurt to meet him for only a minute to find out his name. What was the harm in that?

≈

Haley scanned Marquette Park as she walked down Fort

Street, along the edge of the park. She stepped onto the grass by the dome-shaped Missionary Bark Chapel and headed toward the statue of Father Marquette in the middle of the park. Marquette had come as a missionary to the local Indians.

She looked around at the few people still milling about. He might not even be here. He may have decided she wouldn't come and left long ago. She hadn't given him much hope. She would make a quick loop through the park, then head home. She didn't want him wasting his time standing around there.

"You looking for me?"

She sucked in a breath and spun around. *The Lone Ranger.*

He raised his eyebrows, daring her to deny it.

She stared at him a moment and decided to ask a question of her own. "What is your name?"

"Is that why you came? Just to find out my name?"

She shrugged and began walking. "I was curious. You do have a name, don't you?"

He walked alongside her. "If I tell you my name, your curiosity might be satisfied and you'll abandon me. Let me buy you a soda or some fudge, and I'll tell you when we're through."

"You're persistent." She headed for the edge of the park.

"Do we have a deal?"

She jumped down from the three-foot wall at the front corner of the park. "Ice cream cone?" She looked up at him sideways.

He smiled in triumph. "Lead the way."

She led him down Main Street to the best ice cream place on the island. "I'll take a scoop of raspberry sorbet on a waffle cone," she said to the girl behind the counter.

"Make that two *large* scoops."

"I don't need that much."

He opened his eyes wide. "It'll take you longer to eat." He turned to the girl. "Two scoops for her, and I'll take two of Rocky Road."

She turned to the girl. "One." The girl looked from one to the other.

He gave Haley a puppy-dog look. "Please have two."

She couldn't help but cave in with that look. "Fine."

His smile broadened, and he turned back to the girl. "We'll both have two."

Haley liked his smile. It warmed her heart. She held their cones while he paid.

He took his cone. "You want to sit?"

"I sit all day. I'd rather walk."

They headed out the door and down the street.

"Are you enjoying the island?" she asked between licks.

"I am right now." He wiggled his eyebrows.

She tried unsuccessfully to keep a straight face. "Are you always this big of a flirt?"

"You bring it out in me."

"If I can't eat all this, I reserve the right to throw half of it away. And you still have to tell me your name."

His only reply was a shrug of his shoulders. What did that mean? Would he tell her or not if she didn't finish? They walked in silence for a while as they consumed most of their frozen treats.

"You said you lead a Bible study. What are you studying?" He pushed the last of his cone into his mouth and brushed off his hands.

She wished she were finished, as well. "We're discussing what Jesus said and did during the crucifixion week." She bit down another round of the cone. Why hadn't she asked for a regular cone that was smaller? Because she thought she was only getting one scoop.

"I went to a church once where the pastor was giving a series of sermons on that. The words and actions of a man who knows he is going to die are very powerful. Especially when that man is the Lord."

"You don't still go to that church?" She ate quickly as the sorbet was leaking out the bottom.

"I've moved around a lot."

He watched her balance between licking the sorbet, eating the cone, and plugging the hole in the bottom. "You're a master."

She was going to finish this cone so he would have no excuse for not giving up his name. She popped the last of the cone into her mouth and ate it. "I ate it all. Now it's your turn."

"May I stand here and marvel for a moment at your skill?"

"No."

He chuckled. "Brent Walker. Are you going to disappear on me now?"

"Not yet."

He guided her across the street to the beach beyond the library. Across the water stretched the five-mile Mackinac Bridge. Soft waves gently lapped the shore.

"Oh, look at the sunset." The clouds beyond the bridge were orange and pink. "Where are you staying?" Dumb question. It made her sound as though she were interested in him. Well, she was interested, but he didn't need any more encouragement.

He pointed to the lights on the shore at the far left end of the bridge. "I'd say about the twelfth light from the left in the second or third row, with my friend Dalton."

She jerked her gaze to him. "You're staying in Mackinaw City?" She hadn't meant to say it like an accusation.

He nodded. "Is it a crime not to stay on the island?"

She glanced back at the city, then at an incoming ferry. "No, but—" She flipped her wrist up to look at her watch, then pointed to the incoming ferry. "That might be the last ferry of the night. You'd better hurry."

She hurried alongside him to the dock. The ferry was tied to the moorings already. "You have your ticket?"

"What if I miss it?"

She turned. He had stopped a couple of paces back.

"Then you'll have to find a vacancy at one of the hotels."

"What if they're all full?"

"Then you'll have to find someone who lives on the island to have pity on you and take you in for the night."

He closed the gap between them. "Is that an offer?"

Her stomach flipped. "No."

He brushed a stray strand of hair back from her face. "Good."

Her stomach did a double flip. "You're impossible." She walked over to where he needed to board. "You'd better get aboard before it leaves without you."

He turned to the boy working the ferry. "How long do I have?"

"Only about a minute," the youth said.

He turned back to her and studied her face a moment. "I'll see you tomorrow."

"Not likely."

"I can buy a whole day's worth of tickets again."

"You do that. But I won't be driving."

His eyes widened. "Your day off?" She nodded once. "Spend some of it with me."

"No. You need to get aboard."

Brent took a step backward toward the ferry. "Please. At least meet me for breakfast."

"I sleep in on my day off."

"Lunch then." He retreated another step.

"No."

"If you're coming, you must board now," the ferry worker said.

Brent climbed aboard and stood at the short length of railing near the back. "I believe you will come. I'm catching the first ferry over, and I'll wait on the dock for you. All day if I have to."

"I told you I sleep in on my day off."

The ferry began to move. "Then dream about me waiting for you on this dock—all day."

She shook her head. He wouldn't *really* wait all day for her. "I'm not coming," she called.

"All day," he called back. Then the ferry was out of shouting distance.

He was impossible. If he wanted to spend his day sitting on the dock, that was his business. He wouldn't really. . . . *All day?* She shook her head again and turned to leave. She stopped short when she saw Shane leaning against the wall of the ferry's dock office. As she approached, he shook his head and shoved off the wall.

"I knew you'd meet him."

"You followed us?"

He walked beside her. "It was either risk your anger for following you or live with guilt if you were wrong and the guy hurt you. I decided I couldn't live with the guilt. Are you mad at me?"

"No. But you could have followed me back, and I never would have known you were there; then you wouldn't have had to risk my anger."

He threw his head back. "I wish I'd have thought of that. I was worrying the whole time you'd never speak to me again and that I'd get caught." They turned up the street and headed toward Haley's dorm. "So are you going to meet him tomorrow?"

She stopped short. "You were eavesdropping on us, too?"

He turned to her. "You guys were shouting back and forth. It was kind of hard not to hear you."

"Oh." She started walking again.

"Do you think it's a good idea to meet him tomorrow?"

"You obviously heard me tell him I wouldn't."

"But you will." He shoved his hands into his pants pockets. "Just like tonight."

"Why do you think that?"

"Because it's who you are. If you know someone is waiting for you or expecting something from you, even if you don't want to, you'll do it. It's the same reason you'll go back to your family in the fall. You know they need you and are expecting you to return."

"If that is true, then why haven't I gone back home already?" Shane was a good friend to talk to. He was mature enough in his faith, even at eighteen, and gave sound advice without pushing. And best of all, he didn't seem to have a crush on her, which made it easier to be his friend.

"Because you made a commitment to stay here until the middle of October."

"A lot of people leave before then. That's why they give a bonus to get people to stay till the end of the season. I could leave."

"Because a lot of people leave is why you won't. They'll need you, and you promised to stay. You won't leave them high and dry."

"How can you be so sure? I left my family to fend for themselves."

"You left them because you were upset. If you hadn't made the commitment here before you cooled down, you would have gone back. Am I right?"

She hated to admit it. "Yes." As much as her family drove her crazy, she felt a responsibility to them. And it wasn't a family member who drove her away. At least he wasn't family yet. She didn't want to think about her family or the reason she fled; she would only wonder how they were doing and feel guilty for not being there for them. They had to grow up sometime.

She cleared her mind of them and turned it back to Mackinac and her life here. "Jason was in a mood tonight."

"He's just territorial."

She twisted her gaze to him. "He's what?"

"Territorial."

"I know what you said. What's it supposed to mean?"

He shrugged. "He saw you first, and he doesn't like someone else moving in on his territory."

"I am *not* his *territory*."

"He thinks you are."

"Shane, have I done anything to encourage him? I try not to. Be honest."

"You're a really nice person. If anything, you ignore him a little, not rudelike or anything. He doesn't want to see that there's nothing between you two. And you're pretty, too."

She smiled at that. "Thanks."

"Um. You do know the Lone Ranger has a thing for you?"

"I figured that one out. And his name is Brent Walker."

"Just checking. Sometimes girls can't read guys, and guys definitely can't read girls. If I could read only one girl, I'd be a much happier Joe."

"One in particular? Do I know her?"

"No. It was over before I came here." He stopped at the door to her building. "Here you go."

"Thanks for walking me back."

"Be careful tomorrow."

"I'm not even planning to meet him."

Shane smiled and walked away.

Well, she wasn't planning on it. She was sleeping in. And if Brent Walker wanted to sit on the dock, so be it. She would not feel guilty.

≈

Brent climbed into his truck and stared out at the nearly empty parking lot. Of all the stupid things to say, "Is that an offer?" topped the list. She should have slapped him. Why had he said it? It just came out. Was he subconsciously trying to gain insight into her character?

"Even a fool is thought to be wise if he keeps silent." Lord, I have likely removed all doubt in her mind of my foolishness. If You would wipe that one comment from her mind and have her not hold it against me, I'd really be grateful.

He hoped she would be at the dock and he'd have another chance. He desperately wanted another chance. But why? He hardly knew her.

six

Haley watched the first ferry of the day dock. She still wasn't sure it was a good idea to meet him today; but he intrigued her, and she wanted to know more about him. Okay, so Shane was right. She couldn't stand the thought of someone waiting for her, expecting her. She had awakened early and couldn't stop thinking about Brent. . .and his waiting for her. She would point him to some great sights and be on her way. Maybe breakfast, but that was it.

Goose bumps rose on her bare legs. It was cooler down by the water than she'd expected. She probably shouldn't have worn her denim skort, but she got so tired of wearing long jeans every day to work with the horses. The weather would warm up, and she'd be glad for the skort.

She pulled her little white cardigan tighter over her pink T-shirt and folded her arms. She watched several passengers disembark before she laid her sights on his navy-fleeced shoulder and arm and then on him. He spoke briefly to one of the workers; a moment later, he saw her, and his mouth spread into a smile. His fleece hung open over a gray T-shirt and olive green walking shorts, his bleach-tipped hair in a handsome disarray.

He maneuvered past the crowd and over to her. "You came."

"It's not what you think." The last thing he needed was encouragement. "I was awake early, so I came down to tell you what sights you shouldn't miss."

He rested both hands on his camera case hanging from his shoulder. "So what are the must-sees I haven't already seen?"

She rattled off several places and where to get tickets or how to get there. Though he was listening intently, she had the impression he didn't care about sightseeing. She wasn't sure what to make of him.

"Last call," one of the ferry workers said.

Then Brent finally spoke. "Have you had breakfast?"

She wasn't sure if she should answer, but she did. "No."

He took her hand, pulled her aboard the ferry, and handed two tickets to the worker. The worker tore off the end stubs and returned them while another worker closed the docking ramp.

"What are you doing?"

"Taking you to breakfast." Soon the ferry was moving.

A mild panic rose in her. Jason's voice echoed in her head. *He could be a stalker.* "The island has plenty of places to eat." And the island was a confined and relatively safe place. But the mainland went on forever.

"I thought we'd eat in Mackinaw City. This way I can be with you without being stared at as if I'm a criminal, and we won't be followed."

She looked at him sharply. "Followed?"

He nodded. "Last night."

Shane. "You saw someone?"

"No, it was more a sense of a presence."

"So you don't actually have proof we were followed."

"I do now. Your look confirmed everything I suspected. So who was it?"

No sense denying it. "Just a friend. He wanted to make sure I was all right." She rubbed the sleeves of her sweater to warm her arms a bit.

"Let's get you inside" He led her inside on the first floor deck to a booth. She sat but didn't scoot in enough to leave room for him. He didn't even hesitate and sat across the table from her as if that were his plan all along. Maybe it was.

"Would you like my jacket?"

"No, thank you. I'm fine." Being out of the chilly breeze made all the difference.

He stretched his arms across the back of the seat. "Did you ask your friend to follow us?"

If she had to come up with one word to describe Brent Walker, it would be persistent. "What difference would that make?"

"It will tell me a lot about you."

"Like what?"

"Well, if you asked him to keep an eye on me, it tells me you aren't sure about me yet and I need to gain your trust. If you didn't ask him to follow us, I won't go so far as to say you trust me, but it tells me at least you don't think I'm out to harm you. So was it your idea or his?"

"I didn't even know he was there until the ferry left and I saw him standing there. But I still don't know about you yet."

He nodded as if approving, then leaned forward on the table. "What can I do to relieve your fears?"

"I just don't know you very well."

He held his arms open. "What do you want to know? My life's an open book."

If that was meant to comfort her, it didn't. She always suspected that people who said something like that had something to hide, and that by saying it, the other person would automatically trust them. "How did you become a Christian?"

"You cut right to what is most important. I'll expect your

testimony when I'm finished. Where to begin?"

Testimony. That was not the word an average person would use if he were not a Christian. *Lord, help me to discern if Brent is for real or not.*

He rubbed his hand across his five o'clock shadow. "My parents were always Bible-thumping Christians and took me to church every Sunday. One Easter, when I guess I was about six, Mom asked me if I understood what it was about. I knew it wasn't about the Easter bunny—Mom had taught me that—so I said something like Jesus died and came back to life. She praised me for my answer. I still remember the smile on her face." He paused as if he were seeing her now. "She explained to me that Jesus died to forgive sins, but He overcame sin when He rose from the dead. Then she explained how everyone does bad things and that I had done bad things. She asked me if I wanted Jesus to take away my sins. I remember not quite understanding everything but being afraid of not going to heaven, so I asked Jesus into my heart."

The simple faith of a child. That wasn't made up. It had to be real. *Thank You, Lord.* "Your mom must be proud of you."

"I'll never know. By the next Easter, Mom was gone—a drunk driver hit her. Dad and I went to church sporadically until he died the day after I turned sixteen."

"I'm sorry."

He nodded and went on. "The lawyer who handled Dad's will recommended I become emancipated. I thought, great, no weird adult strangers telling me what to do. Dad and I had been playing music gigs since I was thirteen. I'd had a pretty carefree lifestyle and didn't look forward to restrictions. I finished high school and wandered for a while in life. On my twenty-first birthday, I straggled into a church, the first since

Dad's funeral. I rededicated my life to the Lord, and I've stuck pretty close to Him ever since."

Wow. What a life he'd had. He could have stopped with his conversion as a child, but he had gone on and been open about his struggles. Showed her his faith was his own and he wasn't imitating his mom's religion. Unlike Jason.

"Your turn."

"My parents and sister are about as close to being Christians as this boat we're on." Right now she felt more connected to this relative stranger than she did her own family. A spiritual connection.

"So who introduced you to Jesus?"

She smiled at the thought. "Julie. She was a girl in high school we all called a Jesus freak. I had no clue at the time how normal and grounded she was. We mostly tolerated her when she talked about God and ignored her the rest of the time. The summer between my junior and senior year, she invited me to a church camp. My family was driving me crazy, so it was either church camp or run away from home. I figured I could always run away after the camp, and it sounded as if it could be fun. I felt so loved and welcomed by everyone at the camp. One morning, I got up before anyone else and took a walk. I knew Julie had something I didn't have; she had a peace and something that came from deep inside her, something real and solid. I wanted what Julie had. I asked the Lord to make me like Julie. I didn't understand at the time that I was asking Jesus to be my Savior. But I do now, and I've never been the same since that first encounter with God. Julie and I became best friends, and I never did run away."

"Until now."

She smiled. "Until now."

He leaned forward. "So why did you?"

Very persistent. "I told you. My family."

"But you left out that final thing—or should I say, person—that caused you to take flight."

She didn't want to go there, not with him. "I thought I was the one who was supposed to ask you questions?"

He gave her a little salute. "Ask away."

"You said you played gigs with your dad. So you're a musician?"

"Of sorts. No professional training. Everything I know I learned from Dad."

"What do you play?"

"Guitar, electric, acoustic, bass, and I can keep a mean beat on the drums. But mostly electric guitar. Drums are a little hard to carry around."

Someone who could understand her musically? The connection strengthened.

"Where is a good place to eat in Mackinaw City?" Brent asked.

"How would I know? I only passed through on my way to the island. I think I was in Mackinaw City all of twelve minutes in early May."

"You haven't left the island since May?"

She shrugged. "I haven't had a reason to." It seemed so remote and removed from her troubles that it was easy to forget.

"A couple of places looked good. We'll pick one and hope for the best."

It wasn't long before the ferry docked and they were walking through the parking lot. People often said it was warmer on the mainland, only by a few degrees, but that slight boost in temperature did seem to make a difference.

He stopped in front of a silver, extended-cab pickup with a canopy covering the truck bed and unlocked the passenger-side door, holding it open for her.

She stared at his truck. How long had it been?

"Would you feel more comfortable if you drove?" He dangled the keys in front of her.

She looked at the keys, then at him, and then back at the truck. "It's not that. I was just thinking how long it's been since I rode in a motorized vehicle."

"You've been stuck on a carless island for three and a half months."

"I wouldn't say *stuck*. Sequestered, tucked away. It's going to feel weird after driving carriages every day for over three months." She climbed in.

He went around, climbed into the driver's seat, and started the engine. When the stereo blasted, he quickly turned it down to almost nothing. "Sorry about that."

"That's okay. You don't have to turn it off." She had felt the bass reverberating in the seat back. "I haven't heard much music since being on the island. What do you have?" She leaned over the center divider and thumbed through his CDs. She had most of these Christian artists. *Same taste in music.* "May I hear this one? I love Steven's music."

He took the CD and put it into the high-end stereo. "I'll turn the bass down a little. Most people don't like to feel as much bass as I do." He reached for the equalizer mounted under the dashboard.

She put her hand on his to stop him. "Don't. I like bass."

He pulled his eyebrows together. "I'll back it off just a bit."

The music vibrated through the cab, filling the space. She missed music. She hadn't brought any with her when she left. She played the organ at the church on her days off occasionally but didn't get to play regularly. She hadn't planned on being gone this long. She hadn't planned anything. Now her fingers were itching for a keyboard.

She turned to him. "What do you have in here?"

He looked over the back of the seat.

She did the same. The seats that normally would have been in the extended part of the cab had been replaced with speakers. A lot of speakers from the look of the grill fronts.

"I have a pair of fifteen-inch woofers, a couple of eights for the mid-range, and two three-inch-wide dispersion dome mid-ranges coupled with two high-compression horn tweeters."

"It sounds great." She leaned back in her seat, careful not to jab her hair clip into her head, and closed her eyes, feeling the music pulsate through her body. She drank it in, then soon realized the truck wasn't moving. She opened her eyes. They were still sitting in the parking lot. "I thought we were going to breakfast."

"I'm enjoying watching you enjoy my system."

❧

Breakfast was satisfying, and Brent drove to the first of many tourist traps on the mainland where he planned to take Haley and parked. Since she was a tour guide, she didn't get to relax as a tourist. But today she would. And these were sights she likely hadn't seen. She didn't seem nervous with him anymore. Had he broken through a barrier with her? He left his jacket in his truck, and she left her sweater.

"Where are you taking me now?"

"Sightseeing. I thought you might like being on the other side of the coin."

"I've seen plenty of sights on the island."

"But does the island have a house of mirrors?" He led her between some buildings that looked as if they came straight from Disneyland, cobblestone walkway and everything. He'd hurry her past the shops.

"Oh. These are the cute Mackinaw shops I've heard about. Can we go in some?"

He wasn't fast enough. "What about the house of mirrors?"

"After that, can we?"

"Sure." He hoped she would forget, and then he'd be off the hook.

He paid their admission, and they were each given a pair of plastic gloves for wearing to keep their fingerprints off the mirrors. The kind of gloves that were thin, clear, and too big for one's hands. He held back the curtain to let Haley enter and followed close behind. Red and green lights reflected off white archways with gold-painted designs. He looked directly at an archway and could see a tunnel extending far beyond what this small building could hold. A dozen or more tunnels branched off and curved around to the right and left. All around them.

Haley put her hands out in front of her and felt around for an opening to find her way. He followed.

His hands soon began to feel sweaty inside the thin, clear plastic, but no problem. If he looked at the carpet, he could avoid every mirror without touching one and tugged off the gloves.

"What are you doing? You're not supposed to take those off."

"More correct, I'm not supposed to get fingerprints on the mirrors, and I won't."

"How—by standing in one place?"

"It's simple. Look down." Though the pattern on the triangle wedges of carpet was carefully designed to look like a mirror image, even when butted against another piece of carpet, the mirrors revealed where they were. "The plastic strips joining the carpet triangles give it away. It's a single flattened half-round where carpet meets carpet but has a line down the middle where the mirror reflects the quarter-round strip." He pointed to the bottom of one of the mirrors. "See—that one's a mirror, and that one, but there is your opening." He stepped over the threshold to a new carpet triangle, turned around, and held out his hands. "See?"

She simply stared at him.

Did she realize her mouth was hanging open?

She touched the mirror on one side of the archway post with one hand and put her other hand through the opening, then stepped across the threshold. She turned around, looking down at each joining strip in turn, calculating the opening. Her gaze slowly rose to him. "That's cheating."

"Because I figured out the secret?"

She put her gloved hands on her hips. "Well, it takes the fun out of it. That's like reading the end of a book to see how things turn out. What is the use of reading the rest if you know how it ends?"

"The Lord didn't think so, or He wouldn't have given us Revelation. Aren't you more comforted knowing Jesus triumphs in the end? I know I am."

She opened her mouth, then closed it; her eyes widened, then narrowed, then widened again.

He waited for her reply.

Her face went through a few more contortions before she said, "You put the gloves back on, and no looking at the floor."

"Do you know how impossible it will be not to look at the

giveaways after you know about them?"

"Willpower."

He held out his hands from his sides. "I confess I have none."

"I believe that. Put the gloves on." She waited while he slipped his hands back into the sweaty plastic. "Keep your head up and your hands out in front of you."

He obeyed, took two steps, then looked down. It was impossible not to.

"No." She stepped in front of him. "Now look at me. Which way?"

He tried to look down, but with her standing in front of him, she blocked his view. But he'd seen the way before she inhibited him. He stepped forward, and she walked backward through the opening.

She nodded. "You already knew that one. Where next?"

It was impossible to tell without looking down. "I don't know."

Her smile broadened. "Pick a direction."

He pointed at random, and she walked backward in front of him. He walked with her until she was backed up against a mirror. He gazed down at her. This was interesting. "You're right. This is more fun."

She held his gaze. "Pick another direction."

"I like this one."

"But it won't accomplish the goal of finding the end." She slid along the mirror to the archway post and around a corner.

One thing he knew was that today he was going to kiss her. He didn't know when, he didn't know where, but he knew how. No preamble, no prelude, no building up to it. No chance for her to turn him down. He would just catch her off guard and kiss her.

He went around the corner in pursuit. There sat six of her in a circle, back-to-back-to-back.

She held out her hands with her palms up. "Which one is the real me? No cheating."

He reached out to the one in front of him and hit a cold mirror.

She laughed softly and waved. "Nope. This one's me."

He reached for the next one and took her hand.

At the end of the maze were four silly mirrors, the ones that made a person look disproportionate, fat or short or stretched way long. He watched Haley make faces into them. She certainly knew how to enjoy a situation and not worry how she looked doing it. But he much preferred the real Haley to the reflections of her. Then they headed back through the maze.

He deftly went through a couple of openings, then turned to see if she was following. Though he couldn't see her directly, he could see her reflection standing firm with her hands on her hips. He peeked back around the corner. "Maybe I should follow you."

She led the way; soon they were back out, and he could take off the plastic. He wanted to hold her hand, but his hands were sticky and wet from the gloves.

The next stop was the restrooms, and he took advantage of it to wash the drying sweat from his hands. When he met her back out in the square, he was about to suggest they head back to his truck and move on to the next sight, but she spoke first.

"I want to go in that shop." She pointed across the cobblestone path to a shop with dresses and stuffed animals in the window.

He refrained from groaning audibly. "I'll wait out here on the bench." He moved toward a seat.

She took his hand and pulled him toward the shop. "Come on. I know, typically guys don't like to shop, but it's not so bad."

To refuse now would be to remove his hand from hers, and he wasn't about to do that. He liked having it in his.

Once inside the store, she took her hand back and picked up some small trinket. "Isn't this cute?"

He gazed at her face. "Cute." She had pulled a bait and switch on him: Take his hand long enough to lure him into the store, then release it once he was trapped. He followed her around as she looked at one trinket after another. Soon she stepped outside, and he drank in the fresh air.

She took him by the arm and guided him into the next shop. He picked at a few knickknacks while she looked around. The next thing he knew, something was plopped onto his head.

"Turn around," Haley said.

As he did, he reached to remove the object from his head.

Haley grabbed both of his hands and pulled them down. "Don't. I want to see it on you." She smiled broadly, then pulled him over to a mirror by a rack of oversized, furry hats in varying bright colors.

Which one had she chosen for him? It didn't matter; he was sure he looked ridiculous. A blue, furry, oversized top hat. Ridiculous didn't quite cover it.

Haley giggled. "It's not really you."

"I could have told you that." He removed it and placed it on her head. "I don't like hats." He ruffled his hair with his hands.

Her claw hair thing didn't allow the hat to sit right on her head. She put it back on the rack. "I'm not a hat person either." She turned back to him and pointed to one side of his head. "Your hair is mussed up on that side."

Though his hair was short on the side, the top was a little

longer and moppy. He ran his fingers through his hair again. "Better?" He never tried to do much with it, just let it sort of scatter where it would, so there wasn't any need to *fix* it.

"Uh-huh."

He gazed into her upturned face. Was this the time? Should he kiss her now? No. It was too early in the day, this place too public. He didn't want to scare her off. Instead, he enjoyed the moment until she turned away and looked at a rack of T-shirts.

She held up a light green one with three kittens on it to herself. "What do you think?"

She was asking him? "It's nice."

She hung it back on the rack and moved on.

Had he said the right thing? Should he have made a bigger deal out of it? He had no practice shopping with a woman, but he wanted to do something to gauge how Haley had taken his comment. "Look at this." He pointed to a fluffy white stuffed cat. She had picked a T-shirt with cats; maybe she'd like this.

She turned immediately. "Oh. It's so cute." She picked it up and petted it.

"I'll buy it for you."

She gifted him with a smile. "I don't want to have it. I just like looking."

She took him in and out of several more shops. He lost count. He was getting pretty good at figuring out what she would like; she favored cats and dolphins.

This shopping thing wasn't so bad. Was it the company? That definitely helped. Maybe it was that shopping was always a solitary act for him—a reminder he was alone in this world except for the Lord. But that wasn't the same as having a flesh and blood person to share things with. And he certainly liked sharing his time with Haley, even shopping.

seven

Once back inside his truck, he said, "So where do you want to go next? There is Colonial Michilimackinac; they do reenactments like at the fort on Mackinac Island. Or Historic Mill Creek, the Mystery Spot, and Old Mackinac Point Lighthouse."

"I don't care. You're the tour guide." She appreciated his being a sport about going into the shops.

"I was rather curious about the Mystery Spot. Sounds mysterious."

He drove across the five-mile Mackinac Bridge to St. Ignace. The rhythmic thump every two or three seconds as the tires rolled over one of the bridge joints shifted to a hum as the left lane changed from pavement to a metal grate. The center archways of the bridge loomed larger. The bridge had been completed in 1957, and every year on Labor Day, some special walk took place across it.

Brent stopped at a diner for lunch before continuing on to the Mystery Spot. After he paid their admission at the gift shop, they joined the group on the steep hillside ready to begin the tour.

"If I could have everyone gather around the flagstone." The petite red-haired guide pointed to a cement block about three feet square on the slanted paved path and waved people closer to her. "The Mystery Spot is the area from the back of the gift shop up the hill, just past the building on the hillside. This area is an anomaly where gravity is defied. If you look in front of me, you will see our flagstone. It marks the entrance into the Mystery Spot."

Haley leaned closer to look as did others in the group.

Brent bent toward her ear. "I'd say a cement slab in the middle of the woods would be a mystery. How did it get here?"

She smiled and jabbed him softly in the ribs. "Be nice. You wanted to come here."

The tour guide continued, "I need two volunteers who are about the same height."

"My brothers are identical twins," said a brown-haired girl of about ten wearing a green plaid sundress. "They're the same height."

A pair of gangly youths, about fourteen, stepped forward.

The guide placed a level on the cement block. "Is the flagstone level?"

The twins looked, and both nodded.

Haley felt Brent move closer to her as the crowd shifted to try to get a look—as if any of them except the twins and the guide could see the bubble in the level.

"Please step up on this side of the stone," the guide said to the twin in the blue T-shirt. She then turned to the one in the orange T-shirt and added, "And you stand on this side." The boys obeyed. The guide looked to the group. "Who is taller?" Everyone in the group agreed that the boy in orange was taller. "Inside the Mystery Spot, people are taller. Now switch places," she said to the boys. "Who is taller now?"

It was incredible. This time the boy in blue looked taller. But Haley knew the two boys couldn't change heights. She knew the Lord could do it in an instant, but she didn't believe He chose to and certainly not as a spectacle.

"Follow me up this way," the guide said.

Haley stopped at the far end of the group with Brent close at her side. Before her stood a slanted wood-planked structure. Though it was built to look like a failing old building, it seemed solid to her.

The guide did a demonstration on the outside of the building with a red ball and water traveling up a shallow trough.

Haley scanned the crowd: a couple of families perhaps, a group of four college boys, and a young couple. But then maybe these groups and pairs weren't even together. They just appeared to be together from her view. To everyone else, she and Brent must appear to be a couple. Though spending time together today, they were not a "couple."

Yet.

Where had that come from? She looked up sideways at Brent. Were they beginning to become a couple? She wasn't looking for a boyfriend but couldn't deny her attraction to him. She kind of liked the idea of being a couple with Brent.

At the doorway, the guide did another demonstration of the strange forces at work, then directed the group inside. "There is a handrail up on your left." Once everyone had filed inside and found their footing on the steeply slanted floor, the redheaded guide talked about the two-foot-high table in the bottom corner of the room, then asked for a volunteer.

Haley wanted to test the waters with Brent a little and grabbed his forearm and raised it.

The guide smiled. "It looks as if you've been volunteered, sir."

Brent gave Haley a good-natured sideways glance and handed her his camera case. "It looks as if I have." He stepped easily up onto the table as directed, leaned off over the front edge, and looked under the table before stepping down. Three more tried to do the same thing before the guide moved on to the next one.

It was strange to see people standing with their feet hanging off the edge of a table and then leaning so far forward they looked as if they should fall but didn't.

Haley again volunteered Brent, but the guide chose others to try to stand up from the chair leaning against the wall at the bottom of the sloping floor. The catch was that they weren't allowed to use their hands to push themselves out of the chair. None of them was successful without their hands. Before the guide moved on, she turned to Brent. "The lady would like you to try this one."

Brent handed his camera case to Haley again and stepped forward. Before he sat in the chair, he gave her a little bow. "Whatever the lady wants." He could no more stand up out of the chair without the use of his hands than the four beefy college boys. All had had to push off the armrests to get up.

"Who would like to try this next one?" the redhead asked.

Brent took Haley by the shoulders and moved her forward. "She does." Turnabout was fair play.

The guide smiled and had Haley sit in a red wooden armchair with the two back legs up on a board nailed six inches or so off the ground. The guide tipped the front legs off the ground and leaned the chair against the wall on the two back legs that were up on the board on the wall. "Have you ever sat in a chair on the wall before?"

Haley shook her head. She could remember getting in trouble for rocking back in her chair at home. Brent snapped a picture.

"Okay. Sit very still and don't move." The guide tipped the chair forward partway and worked it back and forth until it was balanced on just the two back legs on the wall, then took her hands away.

The people watching looked amazed.

Brent snapped another picture.

The little girl with the twin brothers raised her hand. "I want to do that."

"Come on up." The guide returned the chair to its starting position, and Haley stood.

After the girl and another person tried the stunt, the group moved to the next room, and Brent whispered in her ear, "Are you a gullible person?"

"I don't think of myself as one."

"So you get how all this works?"

She understood the trick now and nodded. "Funny how the brain works, but it's still fun."

The redhead did demonstrations in this room, as well. Brent volunteered Haley for every one, and she returned the favor.

The end of the tour exited through the gift shop—one way to get people to buy something before they left. If she walked a little slowly, she could look at quite a few of the souvenirs before she and Brent reached the front exit.

"Do you want to look around a bit?" Brent asked.

She looked up at him surprised. He hadn't exactly enjoyed shopping earlier but had gotten into the spirit of it. "Just a quick once through. I promise not to take long."

"One condition: no hats." Brent followed her around, acting as though he were interested in the variety of souvenirs designed to tempt a person to part with his money. Haley had gone down one side and was on her way up the other toward the exit door when a rack of Christmas ornaments caught her eye. Now these were worth looking at. An ornament was small and useful. Her parents had many ornaments from the various places they'd traveled. She looked at several and had pulled off a coppery one when a wooden, jointed snake wiggled in her face.

"Hiss."

She sucked in her breath and pushed the toy away.

Brent's face contorted as he struggled to hold back a laugh. "Are you afraid of snakes?"

She hung the ornament back on the rack. "Only fake ones that are suddenly thrust into my face." She spun back quickly and reached out to take the snake from him, but he was faster and hid it behind his back. She could try to reach around him, but that would only serve to put her in a similar position as in the house of mirrors. "I'm not foolish enough to think I can actually get that from you."

"But you could try."

Trying would involve standing very close and reaching both hands around him. She wasn't ready to step over that line with him yet. She turned to a bin of batik sarongs. "These are cute."

Brent looked over her shoulder. "What are they?"

"Sarongs."

"Is that *saright*? What do they do?"

She unfolded a blue one with dolphins and wrapped it around her waist. "You can wear it over a swimsuit like a skirt. Or you can wear it like a shawl or scarf or make it into a turban. Some girls even fashion them into a top." She pulled out a yellow one. "You want to try one? It's not a hat. You didn't say anything about sarongs."

"You are too funny." He backed away. "I saw a maze across the road. Do you want to go through it?"

"Sure." She held up the yellow sarong. "I think this could be your color."

He shook his head and backed away another step. "You wait here, and I'll go ask about the maze."

She put back the yellow sarong and took off the blue one, then folded it corner to opposite corner into a triangle and tied it around her waist again at her left hip. She liked it, but she didn't have the money for it today. The cash in her pocket would cover it, but she'd better keep that in case things went south with Brent and she had to get herself back to the island. She could come back on her next day off prepared and get it along with the ornament.

Brent returned. "We're all set to get lost in the labyrinth. You ready?"

She reached for the knot at her hip. "Just let me put this back."

"I thought you liked it."

"I do, but I can't buy it today. I'll come back another time to get it."

"Well, I paid for one today, so you might as well take it."

"You bought this for me?"

"Well, I'm not wearing it."

"Why?"

"It wouldn't look good on me."

She swatted his arm. "Why did you buy it for me?"

"I wanted to." He shrugged. "It's not a big deal. It didn't cost that much."

Even though it was inexpensive, a gift put their relationship on a different level. Did she want to move to another level with him? She didn't *not* want to. "Thank you," she finally said.

"You're welcome. You ready to go get lost?"

She nodded and felt the warmth of his hand rest at her lower back as he guided her out the door and across the road.

eight

Brent followed Haley into the maze tucked in the edge of the forest. Though the sign threatened a guard, there was none to be seen. People were on their honor to pay admission at the gift shop.

As in a real fort, the maze had rustic log planks dividing the pathways. Haley stopped at the T inside the entrance. "Right? Or left?"

"It probably doesn't matter which way we enter. Go in one way and out the other."

"Follow the arrow then." Haley turned left down the first passage. The crushed rock path crunched beneath their feet.

"So you ran away from Mommy, Daddy, Sister, Grandpa, the dog, and who else?"

"I didn't run away from the dog. Tawndy has been gone for several years." She turned right.

He hesitated. Why was she so reluctant to tell him? She had freely told him she ran away, opening herself to the question of why. The more she resisted, the more he wondered. He turned the corner and met her coming back.

"This one's a dead end." She thumbed behind her.

"Why'd you leave home? By not answering, you only make me more curious."

"You are more persistent than a dog with a bone." She moved to slip by him.

He put his hands on the walls on either side of him. "Say

the magic words, and I'll let you pass." He watched her mouth move back and forth as if deciding whether or not to tell him. She took a step backward, and he took a step forward; then suddenly she turned and dashed away. He stood there. *Where does she think she's going?* She had already said it was a dead end. "You're trapped." He heard a giggle and the grinding of the rock path. He walked to the end of the passageway and couldn't believe Haley was crawling under the wall. Turning, he headed back. Could he catch her going through the maze? At the T, he made a fast decision to head back to the beginning. He hid in the entrance alley and waited. Her hurried footsteps grew closer, and he anticipated her arrival.

She came around the corner, skidded to a stop with a squeal, and headed back into the maze. He chased after her and grabbed her arm, pulling her back around to him. This was the moment. He pulled her closer and kissed her. He kissed her long enough to hold her an instant but not long enough for her to get over the initial shock and push him away.

Voices entering the maze crowded the moment, and he pulled Haley aside as the girl and her twin brothers darted past them into passageways. "We almost got run over."

Haley only nodded.

What was she thinking? Had he scared her by kissing her? Now he wished he hadn't done it. The stolen kiss wasn't nearly as satisfying as he had imagined.

He led her out and blinked in the bright sunlight, hoping for some way to break the tension he was feeling. To the right, flags waved over a miniature golf course. "Do you want to play a round of golf?"

"Sure."

She walked with him back across the road to the gift shop, where he paid, and they each received a club and a ball.

On the golf course, they stood at the first hole to putt. "You go first," he said.

Haley set her ball down and prepared to hit it.

What was she thinking about that kiss? She hadn't pushed him away or slapped him. That was good. But he hadn't been able to gauge her reaction either, because of those kids coming into the maze. Now the moment was past, and he had no way to tell. But she was still here with him. He wouldn't worry about it.

Haley putted, and her ball went down and around and stopped near the hole. She smiled at him. "Your turn."

That looked easy enough. He grabbed his club in both hands and hoped he didn't make a fool of himself. He stared down at the ball and prepared to swing.

"Like this." Haley stepped up beside him and held her club out with her hands positioned on the grip.

He held up his hand. "I've got it. I've got it." He had watched how she did it and swung. It was a pathetic putt. How did she made it look so easy? He was afraid to look at her and see a gloating expression or, worse yet, pity, but he did look.

Her back was to him as she prepared to putt. She tapped her ball, and it dropped right into the hole. She plucked it out and turned to him with a shrug.

He took three more hits to get his ball into the hole. The next two holes were similarly miserable.

At hole four, Haley stood in front of his ball with her hands on her hips. "Are you ready to take a little advice now?"

"You've done this before."

"High school golf team."

He hung his head and took a deep breath. It would be foolish not to accept help at this point. "Okay."

She set her club to the side and stood at his right shoulder. She put one fisted hand above the other as if holding an invisible club. "Hold the club like this." He gripped the club as she showed. She leaned in against his shoulder and put her right hand over his. "Just move it a little more this way."

He looked away to smile. He liked her this close. This was too good to be real.

"Now move your left foot forward."

He drank in her closeness, hay and sunshine. This close he could easily kiss her again.

"Are you concentrating?"

"On what?"

"On what I'm trying to teach you."

He hesitated before answering. "I must confess that I'm a wee bit distracted. But I'm paying attention now."

"Line up your shot, then look where you want the ball to go." She grabbed her club and walked down the green, then knelt down and pointed to a spot on the bumper wall. "You want the ball to hit here to make it through this passage on the first shot. You want to just miss the corner."

He lined up with where she said to hit it, took a deep breath, and swung. Too hard. But the ball did miss the corner—and the spot Haley was pointing at—and bounced several times back and forth in the passageway. It then spun off another corner, went down past the hole, bounced off the far wall, and crept back to the center past her ball, and dropped into the hole.

He released his breath and raised his club in the air. "Yes!"

Haley stared at the hole. "I can't believe you made a hole in one off that shot. Good job."

He pulled out the scorecard and marked it down. "I'm catching up now. Watch out."

She removed his ball from the hole and tapped hers in. After retrieving hers, she brought him his ball and pressed it into his palm. "It's going to take more than a fluke."

He looked down at her. "Is that a challenge?"

"I don't think beating you will be much of a challenge." She sashayed off to the next tee.

He smiled. She was flirting back.

As on every other hole, her first hit landed inches from the cup. He lined up his shot.

"Remember to look where you want the ball to go."

He hit the ball. It zoomed past the hole, bounced off the wall, and rolled back toward him, stopping a foot from where it started.

"Tap gently. It's not a baseball." She tapped hers in.

He tapped his ball, and it stopped near the hole. One more tap and it went in. It was obvious he wasn't going to beat her on skill alone, because he had none when it came to golf.

Haley hit a hole in one. It took him three tries to get his ball in.

Haley lined up for the next hole. As she pulled her club back to hit the ball, he hooked her club with his. She swung her head back to look at him, and the hair sticking out of the top of her hair weapon did a little dance. "Do you mind?"

"Sorry." He unhooked their clubs. On her next attempt, he hooked it again. She took it well. And on her third attempt, when she was expecting him to do it again, he didn't, and her shot went wide.

He lined up his shot, then looked at her and swung. He kept his gaze on her as she watched the ball. Her eyes widened, then her jaw dropped. He looked down the green and furrowed his brow. Where did it go? He looked back at his feet, but the ball wasn't there either.

"I can't believe you did that again."

He looked into the hole, and there it was. "Yes!"

Haley took three more hits to sink her ball, and he hadn't done one thing to distract her.

At the next hole, as she prepared her shot, he studied her hair weapon. It had to go. Just when he thought he'd figured out the contraption, Haley swung her head around to look at him.

She squinted and pointed with her club. "Put your club down over there."

He obeyed and did his best to look innocent.

She squinted at him one last time before turning back around to focus on her shot.

He stepped forward and pinched the weapon, and her hair fell free.

She turned and glared at him, then tucked her hair behind her ears and took her shot. A sad shot. She held out her hand. "May I have my hair clip back?"

He looked from the clip to her free hair framing her face. "Nope."

"Fine. I'll win anyway."

He looked to where her ball had stopped. "I wouldn't be so sure about that. You don't shoot so well without this."

"Take your stroke." She walked to her ball to watch. "Or two or three."

His hit was good. Even he couldn't miss sinking it on his next shot.

He poked and tickled her and made noises and faces when it was her turn. She took it all with a smile and a determination to win. And now it came down to the last hole.

She held out her hand to him and wiggled her fingers. "I want to see the scorecard."

He handed it to her. "We're tied. Winner of this hole wins the game."

She handed back the card. "You go first."

"Ladies first."

"I insist. I want to see what I have to beat. I play best under pressure."

He lined up his shot and took a deep breath. Talk about pressure. He turned to her. She might decide to pay him back on this hole. "You mind standing where I can see you?" She did his bidding with a little bow. Was she going to make some loud sound to throw him off? He mentally prepared himself for that and pulled back his club. *Lord, let this be a great shot.* He swung. After bouncing off several walls, the ball stopped a sliver's width from dropping into the hole. *Yes!* He tried not to look smug. "You'll have to get a hole in one to beat that."

She raised her chin slightly and smiled. "So be it."

He wouldn't even heckle her this time. He'd let this hole be fair and square.

She prepared, swung gracefully, and landed her ball right in the hole.

He stared at the black spot that had swallowed her ball. "I can't believe that."

"I believe that makes me the winner. And I didn't even cheat."

"I didn't *cheat*—I *distracted*."

"Are you going to put your ball into the hole, or should I?"

"Are you gloating?"

She tipped her head and thought a moment. "I believe I am.

May I have my hair clip back now?"

"No. You gloated."

"Then take your final stroke so I can officially win."

"What if I don't? Then it looks like a tie."

"If you don't finish, you can't place. And we'd still both know who won. You want a rematch?"

Was there any chance he could beat her fairly? Only if her hands were tied behind her back and she used her mouth to swing the club. "I'll pass." He knocked his ball in, and they returned their clubs to the gift shop.

He opened the passenger door of his truck for her. "I can't believe you won."

She stepped up into the cab. "I must admit I had help on that last hole. I was praying real hard."

"What do you think I was doing the whole game?" He closed her door and climbed into the driver's side. "I think we've done everything there is to do here. Where to now? We still have the lighthouse, the colonial fort, and Mill Creek."

"Surprise me."

"Okay." Where should he take her next? He could take her to Fort Michilimackinac, introduce her to Dalton, then have a nice dinner somewhere and an evening stroll on the beach by the lighthouse. That sounded like a perfect plan to round out the day.

The only shortcoming was that he was running out of pictures on his camera. He hadn't downloaded the recent pictures he took on Mackinac Island, and the memory stick in his camera was nearly full. "Do you mind if I stop by Dalton's house? I'm running out of pictures. It'll only take a few minutes to download them to my computer."

"Sure. That's fine."

He crossed the bridge and headed for Dalton's house in Mackinaw City. The houses on the street were on the small side but nice. He parked out front. "I'll only be a few minutes. I'll leave you the keys so you can listen to music if you want."

He jogged up to the door and let himself in. He flipped open his computer and waited for it to boot. "Come on— hurry up." He didn't want to leave Haley waiting too long. She could decide to leave without him. He strode to the window and peered out at her waiting in his truck. *Don't get restless and disappear on me.*

He went back to his computer and plugged in the cord to both the computer and the camera. Soon the pictures were downloading. He returned to the window, but his truck was empty. He opened the door and took a harder look. She was gone.

He walked outside and looked up and down the street as he strode to his truck. She wasn't there, but her sweater still lay on the seat. He looked back toward the house, then went around the side of it. When he rounded the back side of the garage, he saw her peering in the window of the garage. "There you are."

She jumped back and sucked in a startled breath. "You scared me."

He chuckled. "Sorry. I got a little nervous when you disappeared from my truck."

"Your friend's house is so cute. It reminds me of a dollhouse."

Cute? Leave it to a woman to call a house *cute*. "Two bedrooms, kitchen, and living room. All the basics."

She pointed toward the garage window. "And studio space. I see you two have quite the setup in there."

"You want a closer look?"

"Sure."

He used the house key and opened the outside door to the garage and flipped on the light.

"What kind of guitar do you have?"

"A fat Strat." He motioned toward his sunburst guitar on the stand.

"Play something."

As he picked up his guitar, Haley walked around Dalton's drum set and sat on the stool. He plugged the cord into the guitar, turned on the tube head amp hooked to a four-by-twelve cabinet, and began playing one of the contemporary Christian songs they had listened to in his truck. After a few bars, Haley joined in humming. She was right on key and pitch.

He wished he wouldn't always judge people's vocal abilities, but he couldn't help it with having perfect pitch, his blessing and curse. He could know a person was praising God, but if he heard too many wrong notes, it was difficult to listen and hampered his own worship. But when a voice was clear and pure, he felt more drawn into worshipping the Lord. With Michelle, his gift had been a curse. But he sensed not with Haley.

He transitioned into another contemporary praise song, and Haley continued to hum. He would love to hear her sing. Could he coax her into it?

He brought that song to a close and moved into a traditional hymn. As he began picking out the notes to "Amazing Grace," he sang softly, hoping she would join in.

She closed her eyes and smiled. Then the words began to flow, and she harmonized with him.

Beautiful. He began the first verse again and stilled his hands on his guitar. He softened his voice. He wanted to stop singing altogether just to listen to her but was afraid if he did she would stop, as well. He could listen to her all day. When the last note faded away, she opened her eyes.

He gazed at her. "You sing beautifully."

"Ten years of vocal lessons."

He turned off the amp and unplugged his guitar. "Ten years? Are you a professional singer then?"

"Hardly. I only sing in church and for fun."

He set his guitar back on its stand. "Then why so many years of training?"

She took a deep breath as if reluctant to answer. "My parents."

He sensed her reluctance was that she did not want to bring up her reason for running away. He would leave that subject alone for now. "Your parents wanted you to become a professional singer?"

"No. My parents wanted me to do other things for them. I learned early that I could get what I wanted with a little negotiation."

"You wanted to become a professional singer?"

She laughed. "It had nothing to do with singing. With my parents pulling me to what they wanted, it was my way of being an individual in a family determined to swallow me up. No one else in the family did anything musical, so it made me unique. It gave me an identity."

"Do you play an instrument, as well?"

"Several. I majored in music in college."

He sighed. "Another thing you do better than I do."

"Not better. Different. I stuck with the traditional orchestral and band instruments after piano. I know nothing of electric guitar or drums. My parents did have their limits, and I knew just how far I could push. Drums would have been too much for them."

That seemed like an opening. "Do you want to learn to play something on them?"

Her face brightened. "Could I? Your friend wouldn't mind?"

"Not at all. Pick up the sticks." He pulled a backless blue wooden chair with paint splatters on it up behind the padded stool she sat on and straddled it behind her. She held a drumstick in each fist. He reached around her and put his hands over hers. "Relax your grip. They aren't golf clubs."

He drew in a deep breath. *Hay and sunshine.* He hoped he could concentrate enough to teach her at least a basic beat. "That's the high hat cymbal, and those are the crash and splash cymbals and the ride cymbal. Three tom drums—small, medium, and large—and a snare." He reached around her and pointed to each piece in turn, his arms touching hers. "At your feet are pedals for the bass drum and high hat. Cross your right hand over to the high hat, your left to the snare, and use your right foot for the bass pedal."

"Which one was the snare?"

"Weren't you paying attention?"

"I confess I was a wee bit distracted."

So he could affect her, as well. He wrapped his arms around her. She sank back against his chest. He held her for a few moments in silence, then tapped the rim of the snare drum with his fingers. "This one."

He covered her hands with his and showed her how to keep a simple four-four beat; then he let go and let her continue the beat while he tapped his foot to help her keep the tempo. Once she seemed to have the hang of that, he showed her a three-four beat. She caught on fast.

"Do you want to try something a little more complicated?"

She craned her neck to look back at him. "My throat is

really dry. Could I get something to drink first?"

"Sure. Let's go inside." He followed her inside the house through the joining door, crossed to the fridge, and opened it. Pretty pathetic. "We have root beer, cola, and limeade."

"I'll try some limeade."

He pulled out the pitcher and took down two glasses. "It's a little more tart than lemonade."

"It sounds good."

He poured them each a glass. Dalton couldn't stand his limeade and preferred sweet soda. He gave one to Haley and motioned her into the living room.

"Where is your friend now?"

"He works at the fort here. Did you know the fort was here first, and then they moved it to the island during the American Revolution?"

She nodded. "We've had all sorts of island history drummed into us. Have you been friends long?"

"Since third grade."

She walked around the room. "I sense a feminine touch here and there. Is your friend married?"

"Used to be. Widowed."

"Oh, I'm sorry."

"It's been three years." He leaned against the back of the green recliner.

"How long were they married?"

"Eight months."

"That's so sad." She stood by the empty fireplace.

"Dalton still has a bad day now and then, but he's mostly doing well."

"That's good." She sat on the couch, but before he could do the same, the cell phone in his pocket rang. Should he even bother? He pulled it out and wanted to groan when he read the display. He gave a heavy sigh and looked at Haley.

"Go ahead. I don't mind."

"Thank you. I won't be long." He answered and stepped back out into the garage. "Mr. Jackson."

"Have you found that worthless Mikkelson kid yet?"

"I'm working on it. Mackinac Island employs thousands of people each summer. I don't even know if he's still there."

"Hurry up. Time is running out. I want his signature before the child is born." Mr. Jackson went on to tell him how to do his job, a job he no longer wanted. But he had made a commitment and was determined to follow through until he had no leads left. He looked longingly at the door to the house while only half listening to Mr. Jackson.

nine

Haley blinked her eyes open for a moment, then shut them again. What had she seen? Brent? She opened her eyes.

Brent's mouth spread into a smile. "You're awake."

Haley sat up. "I must have dozed off for a moment."

"A little over an hour."

She widened her eyes. "I was asleep for an hour?"

He nodded.

"Great. Some date I am." She had only meant to rest a bit while listening for Brent to come back inside.

"I can't say you didn't warn me."

She raked her hands through her hair and yawned. "What? I told you I was going to take a nap?"

"The other day when I asked you what you did on your day off. The first thing you said was 'sleep.'"

"I'm really sorry, Brent. Please don't think I consider you boring or anything. Because you're not."

"It just means you're comfortable around me and trust me. That's a compliment." He slid off the green recliner chair onto one knee in front of her. "But since you feel in debt to me at the moment, I'd like to ask you something."

She didn't like what his position insinuated. She wished he would stand up or something.

"Will you. . ." He paused to take a breath.

Haley held hers. He couldn't be. He was bold but not that bold. She stood and faced him.

He stood, too.

That was better.

". . .allow me to kiss you?"

She released her breath. Was that all? "You've already kissed me. Why ask now?"

"That was a stolen kiss. Things stolen are never as rewarding as things freely given." He stepped closer. "I want to know that you want me to kiss you. Because I want to kiss you." He put his hand on her cheek. It was warm and comforting.

The front door opened. "You're here." A brown-haired man, who looked to be around Brent's age, stepped inside with a bag in his arm. "Oops. You're busy. I'll come back later." He turned and walked out.

"Dalton, wait." Brent went to the door.

Was that a "saved by the bell" or a "go away, you're interrupting"? Her cheek cooled quickly where Brent had touched it.

Dalton gave a sheepish grin. "I can tell when I'm interrupting something, and I'm *soo* interrupting."

"Get in here."

Dalton came back inside.

"Dalton, this is Haley. Haley, Dalton. This is Dalton's house."

A shock of dark brown hair hung down on Dalton's forehead. She stepped forward and held out her hand. Dalton shifted the bag and shook her hand.

He turned to Brent. "I bought chicken and sides, figuring you wouldn't have eaten. There's plenty for three, but you probably have other plans."

Brent glanced at her.

She smiled. "The chicken smells great. I'm starved."

⋆

After eating and helping clean up, Haley said to Dalton, "I noticed you have an electronic keyboard out in the garage. Would you mind if I played it?"

Dalton gave Brent a quizzical look. Brent nodded. Then Dalton said, "Sure." He led the way out into the garage and turned it on. "It works pretty much like a piano but has many more features."

Dalton was cute. He was trying to be gracious but wasn't sure how to instruct her in using the instrument. "I have the model just before this one."

Dalton sighed, and his shoulders relaxed. Should she tell him she had played the drums she knew nothing about? No sense worrying him.

What should she play? Something she hadn't felt she could play on the organ in the church on the island. She picked the settings and turned to Brent and Dalton. They both looked at her in anticipation; what was this stranger going to play? "Do you both know 'The Wonderful Cross'?"

Dalton smiled and jumped to his seat at the drums, and Brent lifted his guitar strap over his head, plugged the guitar in, and turned on the amplifier.

Since she was around musicians, she saw no sense in playing alone. She played the opening bars and began singing. Brent jumped in on guitar. She could see Dalton waiting his entrance. She was glad when she reached the chorus and Brent and Dalton joined in. Obviously these two had played the song together many times before. The second time the chorus came up, she closed her eyes and lifted her praise to the Lord. The one drawback to playing an instrument was that she couldn't raise her hands to the Lord.

She opened her eyes at the end of the song.

Dalton looked giddy. "Do you know 'Every Day'?"

The three of them obviously had the same taste in music. She nodded and made her selections on the keyboard. "Are you singing lead?"

Dalton nodded and ripped off the opening beat. She and Brent jumped in. Dalton's voice was clear and steady despite drumming. She joined in with Brent on the chorus. Toward the end of the song, she backed off on vocals and listened to Brent and Dalton harmonize, then came back in.

"You two have done that one a lot. Do you play someplace on a regular basis?"

"Not anymore," Brent said.

"Why not?"

Dalton shrugged. "We grew up?"

"That's a shame." She turned to Brent. "It looks like it's your turn to pick a song and sing lead."

Brent shook his head. "Dalton's the lead between us."

"I heard you earlier. You can sing lead fine. Pick something."

He smiled. "Okay." He turned a knob on his amp and pressed an effects pedal with his foot. "Let's switch artists. Do you know 'Shine'?"

Brent played the opening bars. His guitar had taken on a distinctly distorted sound. Then Haley and Dalton joined in. Haley didn't know the song well enough to play the melody, so she just filled in with some chords and the low end. Brent's voice had a rougher edge than when he sang earlier, but it sounded good and fit the song.

When the song was over, she looked at her watch. Time to go. "As fun as this has been, I have a ferry to catch."

"It's that late already?" Brent looked at his watch, then

switched off his amp and unplugged his guitar. As they walked through the house, she could hear Dalton playing a beat on the drums.

Once outside, she rubbed her upper arms. "The temperature sure cools off after sunset."

"Where's your sweater? In the house?"

"No, I think I left it in your truck."

He opened the passenger door, then held her sweater for her to slip into.

"Thank you." She climbed in.

He stepped in and drove to the dock.

"We didn't get to those other sights you wanted to take me to."

"I'll just have to kidnap you for the day again next week."

She liked the sound of that. The next six days were going to drag in anticipation.

At the ferry dock, Brent helped her out of his truck and handed her a ticket. "Thank you for spending the day with me."

"I had a great time. Thank you."

Brent held her hand as he walked her to the end of the dock where others waited for the last ferry to the island that night. She stopped short of the end of the meager line and faced him. "Yes."

He stared at her a moment, then raised both his eyebrows. "Did I miss something? I thought I was paying attention."

"My answer is yes."

His eyebrows worked together to pinch the skin between them. "Did I ask a question?"

She tried to hold her smile in check and nodded.

"I guess my mind drifted. When did I ask this question?"

"Earlier today." She wanted him to remember the question on his own.

He dropped his shoulders and tipped his head sideways. "I must have asked a lot of questions today. But you're not going to tell me, are you?"

Nope, she wasn't going to tell him, but she definitely wanted him to get it. "I'll give you a hint. It was at your friend's house. . .just before he came home."

His confused expression morphed into a pleasant smile. "Just to make sure I understand correctly, I'll ask again." He stepped closer and cupped her face in his hands. "May I kiss you?"

Her insides flipped, and she whispered, "Yes."

He pressed his lips to hers.

The blare of the ferry horn startled them apart.

"I have to go." She didn't want to.

He gazed at her a moment longer. "I'll see you tomorrow."

She put her hands on his and took his hands from her face and squeezed them. "You don't have to ride in my carriage. I'll meet you for lunch at the Yankee Rebel. Do you know where that is?"

"I'll find it."

She reluctantly released his hands and boarded the ferry. She chose a window seat on the first deck and looked for him on the dock. He was quickly walking back its length toward the ticket booth, then disappeared behind the structure. Her heart ached to see him hurrying away. Once out of sight, she untied her sarong, unfolded it, and retied it the long way over her legs to keep them warmer. She sat leaning against the window and stretched her legs out on the bench seat. She looked at her watch. The ferry wouldn't disembark for another five minutes. Why hadn't she stayed on the dock with Brent until the last possible moment? It was what he'd done last night. She closed her eyes and leaned her head back against the cold glass. It had been a wonderful day.

Soon the ferry began to move.

"Is this seat taken?"

She popped her eyes open and saw Brent. "The ferry's pulling out." She swung her feet to the floor.

"I know." He scooted onto the bench next to her.

What was he doing? "This is the last ferry for the night."

"Going to the island. But it'll be coming back."

"You're riding the ferry over just to stay aboard and ride it back."

"That was too sweet a kiss to let it be cut short by the ferry's horn." He cupped her cheek and leaned forward.

She met his lips.

After a moment, he pulled back. "That was much better." He slipped his arm around her shoulders and settled in beside her. "I wasn't ready to say good night."

She shook her head. "You have sent my head spinning. I can't believe you are riding the ferry just to be with me."

"Why not?"

"I don't know. People don't do that. It would be a waste of their time." She could easily name a half-dozen people close to her who wouldn't do it. But she doubted if she could name one besides Brent who would.

"This is how I want to spend my time right now, so it is anything but a waste."

She relaxed against his side. This was where she wanted to be, next to him. How could she know that after one day? *Lord, is this real?* Or was it some rebound thing? It had been nearly four months. Certainly she had recovered somewhat.

Brent squeezed her closer and kissed the side of her head. He was riding the ferry just to be with her a few more minutes. How romantic was that? "I can't believe I feel like this about you after only one day."

"We actually met four days ago. And if you add it up, it's been longer than you think."

She shook her head. "How can four days be longer than four days?"

"If your average date lasts two to four hours, then today has been the equivalent of at least four dates." He took her hand and held it. "And last night's ice cream, though it wasn't that long, was a prearranged meeting, so it counts. And all day with you in the carriage has to count. We'll call it two more dates. And I saw you off and on for the first two days. That has to count for something. And I thought about you in between."

She had thought about him, too. Nice, pleasant thoughts.

"So in total, it's as if we've been on—let's say—ten, plus dates. That could normally take a couple of months. You can get to know someone fairly well in that time. We just cut out all the in-between time the rest of life takes up."

"You really know how to put a spin on things."

"I want to assure myself I haven't lost my mind."

"Are you saying I make you crazy?"

"Nope. But I'm crazy about you."

She felt as though her emotions were out of control. They were taking her along on some fantastic ride, and she never wanted to get off. She liked the warm, comfortable feelings but wondered how long they would last before they crashed. Maybe Brent was different. Maybe Brent would last.

He kissed the side of her head again. "Does our age difference bother you?"

"Age difference?"

"I'm guessing you're college age, early twenties. Earning money to finish school. I'm thirty-two. That makes a ten-year spread. Does that bother you?"

Should she tell him her age? Or tell him she didn't mind their age difference? "There's only a seven-year difference. That's not so much." Funny how it seemed like a yawning gap with Jason, practically a generation gap, but nothing with Brent.

Brent turned to face her, and his eyes widened. "Twenty-five? Really?"

"You're pretty quick with math."

"They do say math and music go hand in hand. So you don't mind the difference?"

"It's not much of a difference. Do you mind?"

"Not at all. I'll confess I've felt as if I've been floundering my whole life. Like a compass spinning round and round with no direction. But you have stopped that. You're my north."

"Shouldn't the Lord be your guiding direction?"

"He is, but He uses people to accomplish His will."

She bristled at that. Even the thought of God using her made her uncomfortable. It shouldn't, but it did. She didn't like the feeling of being someone's puppet. But she liked the idea of being the one person who could help another. That she was truly special to someone. . .to Brent.

The ferry docked, and Brent walked her onto the dock. "I wish I could walk you home."

"I'll be fine."

"It's not for you. It's purely selfish motives on my part. This has been a perfect day, and I don't want it to end."

She didn't either. "We'll see each other tomorrow."

"The Yankee Rebel. I may not be able to wait until lunch to see you. So if you see a familiar face on your carriage, that will be me." He hurried to board the ferry before it departed.

Haley watched until the ferry was out of sight. She took a deep breath to savor the moment.

She should have told him not to buy a ticket, that if she had an extra seat, he could ride for free. If the seat wasn't taken anyway, she saw no harm.

She turned around and stopped short, sucking in a breath.

Jason glared at her. "You left the island with him and spent all day with him? You know nothing about him."

"That's what spending the day was all about, getting to know one another."

"He could be some psycho."

She was getting tired of Jason's possessiveness. "He isn't though."

"What if he's simply trying to gain your trust, then drags you off someplace and you're never heard from again?"

"He's not like that. I trust him."

He grabbed her shoulders. "What about us?"

His forcefulness was scaring her. She shook free. "There is no *us*—never has been. I don't feel that way for you."

"But you do for him." He shook his head and stormed off.

She never meant to hurt him. She had no control over his emotions. If she did, she'd direct them elsewhere.

"Ignore him."

She spun around. "Shane."

"You couldn't have done anything about Jason."

After Jason's outburst, she was relieved to have Shane's company. "I feel bad for him. He's a nice guy and all."

"He'll get over it. It's like learning your mom and dad are Santa Claus. It takes awhile to adjust to the truth."

She retrieved her bike and walked in silence beside him. Why did relationships have to be so complicated? Why did

Jason have to like her? *Lord, help Jason understand. Help him look to someone else or focus on his new life at college.*

"Did you have a nice day?"

His question pulled her out of her funk over Jason. She smiled. "A very nice day. He surprised me by taking me to the mainland. He took me to breakfast, and then we saw some sights and ended up back at his friend's house and had a short jam session."

Shane was quiet for a moment, then asked, "What's he like? Would I approve of him?"

"Approve?"

He nodded. "I'm playing big brother here, even though I'm younger than you. I want to make sure this guy is good enough for you."

That was sweet of him. "He seems wonderful. He's a neat Christian, and I believe he truly loves the Lord. It's not a facade or an act. He's funny and makes me smile. I want to be wherever he is. Isn't that silly after so short a time?"

"He's captured your heart."

"I'm not sure about that. It's all so sudden. I wasn't looking for anyone."

"Isn't that the way love is? When we aren't looking, it sneaks up on us, and we're helpless."

"Oh, I wouldn't say 'love.' We've only spent one day together." She wouldn't try to explain how it had seemed like more, as Brent had done. She would be seeing him tomorrow. "Shane, if you really want to play my brother, have lunch with us tomorrow. We're meeting at the Yankee Rebel. I know you'll like him."

"Will you allow me to give you my honest opinion?"

"That's what I want." She could use counsel from a good Christian friend.

"Even if it's negative?"

"I trust your judgment. If you see something in him I'm too blind to see, I want to know." She could have used a friend like him before.

He stopped at the door to her dorm and waited while she locked her bike to the rack. "I'm going to see if Jason is around. I'll talk to him, help him understand."

She put her hand on his arm. "Thank you."

She went to her room and dressed for bed. She was tired. She didn't normally do so much on her day off. But it was a good tired. As she lay in bed, Brent's face danced through her head. She was special to him. His north. But how could she be a directional guide for Brent when she didn't even know where she was going after the middle of October when her job on the island was through? How scary to have him looking to her for direction. Maybe he could be her north, as well, and they could find their way together. They could figure it out with the Lord.

૨૪

When Brent walked through the front door, Dalton lay stretched out on the couch with his hands behind his head. The beat Dalton had been playing on the drums when Brent left was a contented beat unlike the abuse he'd been giving them a few nights ago. The short jam session had been good for him.

"Hey, you're in my bed."

Dalton smiled broadly but didn't move. "She is so your type."

"You think so?" He made a fist and brought it to his chest. "She does something to me here."

"Let me know when the wedding is."

"I've only known her four days. I'm hardly prepared to make that kind of decision."

"I hear bells ringing from the church steeple."

Is she the one, Lord? Finally.

"Do you think my having no permanent residence is too weird?" He'd never worried about that before. "I've rented an apartment now and then for a short while."

Dalton unclasped his hands from behind his head and sat up. "You're free to go where the Lord leads you. You haven't put down stubborn roots that may be keeping you in a place the Lord may not want you. You aren't afraid to look up and move on."

So Dalton was struggling, too, with his place in this world. Was there ever a time a person could be sure? Maybe he had been avoiding settling down in one place because he was afraid it had nothing to offer him.

"Do you think it will scare Haley off?"

"Your lifestyle is unconventional—that's true. But maybe the Lord is pairing you with Haley for that reason. Maybe that's what she's looking for—someone who doesn't fit into the same mold as everyone else. I never thought I'd settle down until I met Joslin. Now I'm an immovable object. Look at Moses. He ran away and lived in the desert for decades. It turned out to be a training ground for something bigger in his life. I don't know why the Lord gave me Joslin for such a short time and then took her away, but I think I'm a better person for having known her."

Dalton leaned forward, resting his forearms on his thighs. "Maybe the Lord has used your mobility to bring you here—to meet Haley. Maybe she's the one to get you to settle down. Or maybe you're the one to set her free from a conventional life."

"I hardly think driving a tour carriage is conventional."

"What about when the season is over? What will she be going back to?"

And what had she run away from? Dalton made it sound as though Brent was a shining knight set out to rescue a beautiful damsel. Though Haley was beautiful, a shining knight he was not.

The phone in his pocket rang. Mr. Jackson again. He turned it off. Nothing had changed from earlier. He was still no closer to finding Justin. "Dalton, would it be irresponsible of me to quit looking for Justin Mikkelson altogether?" Dalton was always a good second conscience for him, helping him stay on the right track.

"Because of Haley?"

"Because I think Mr. Jackson is an overbearing brute. He treats his daughter like a possession, a possession that has seriously disappointed him by making him look bad. She was probably desperate to find love and acceptance and found it in Justin's arms."

Dalton stood and stretched. "Do you think he's on the island?"

"It's likely."

"Do you think you can find him?"

"Given enough time, probably."

Dalton clasped him on the shoulder. "Then to quit would be irresponsible."

He knew that. He'd needed it confirmed.

"I'm going to bed. I have a war to fight tomorrow, and I believe we'll win." Dalton headed for his bedroom.

He should get some sleep, too, but wanted to see Haley one last time before going to bed. He turned on his laptop and looked through the pictures he'd downloaded earlier. He had taken pictures all day long, and Haley hadn't seemed to mind. He wanted to spend time with her, but he had a job to do.

He needed to get serious and find this Justin and be done with it. And it was obvious he couldn't do it alone. He needed help. Should he ask Haley? Tell her he'd been working a job and see if she could help him?

ten

Haley rubbed her face once again. She could not wake up this morning after a night of thinking about Brent. It had been after two before she had fallen asleep. The only thing that had gotten her out of bed this morning was the prospect of seeing him again today. Lunch was too far away. Maybe he'd ride as he'd suggested he might. She hoped so. And if she could catch him before he purchased a ticket, she would offer him an empty seat if she had one.

Harry, the stable master, was talking on the phone in the small office in the barn while she made a last check of harnesses and traces. She peeked in the doorway and gave him a thumbs-up that she was heading out, the last to leave. She was generally the first. Harry held up his hand for her to wait. She leaned on the doorframe while he finished his conversation. "I have someone here who I can send right over."

She would be that someone since she was the only one still around. What if Brent was waiting to ride in her carriage? She pulled the scrunchie out of the low ponytail it was holding, finger combed her hair, and put it back in. She preferred her hair clip, but Brent still had that. She hoped he'd bring it today.

Harry hung up and turned to her. "Giff over at the police station needs an extra pair of hands. I told him I'd send you."

Giff was the deputy. She wasn't. What good could she be? "Can't someone else do it?"

"You haven't gone out yet. And when I told Giff I'd be sending you, he said, perfect—he could use someone with a good head on her shoulders. See—you're not just a pretty face."

"But Tom and Jerry are all set to go."

"I'll take care of them. Giff is waiting."

As she turned to leave, she bit her bottom lip. She put on her helmet, straddled her bike, and was off, coasting downhill as fast as she could. As she came into town, she turned down Main Street and swung by the carriage tour ticket office to see if Brent was lingering. She parked at the curb and left the bike to go inside to speak with Jessica. "Has that guy who rode my carriage the day before yesterday been by today?"

"No. He didn't come yesterday either. At least not on my shift."

"I had yesterday off."

"So he was riding just to see you. I hope I didn't get him in any trouble."

"No. It's fine. If he comes by, tell him I'm doing some other business, but I'll see him for lunch."

"Ooo. Is something going on with you two?"

She smiled and shrugged. "Maybe. His name is Brent Walker. Thanks." She turned and peeked in Big John's office. "I'm helping Giff with something. I don't know how long it will take, but when I'm finished, I'll get a carriage."

"Harry already called me. Don't worry about it. Whenever you're through with Giff will be fine."

She headed back out and got on her bike but still saw no sign of Brent. At the police station, she parked her bike and went inside. Alli, the receptionist, motioned her to go right into Giff's postage stamp–sized office. All the offices on the island seemed to be compact. They had no extra space for frills, just the necessities.

Giff sat behind his desk with his hands folded, his wavy red hair tamed neatly in place. She stood at the doorway a moment before he noticed her and waved her inside. He stood. "Come in."

"Harry said you needed my help. I'm not sure what I can do."

He reached for the door. She stepped out of the way so he could close it. "We have a private investigator here looking for someone on the island. You know the island well, so I thought you could show him around." As he stepped back around his desk, he motioned to a man in the chair. "Haley, this is Brent Walker."

Brent stood. His face paled as he stared at her. But no one could be more shocked than she.

Giff went on. "He's looking for a boy named Justin Mikkelson."

She shifted her gaze to the floor. *Justin Mikkelson?* That's why Brent had asked her about him several days ago. He was here on a mission, and it had nothing to do with her—except to use her. She balled her hands into fists until her nails dug into her palms. She couldn't believe what she was hearing.

Unaware of her discomfort, Giff continued. "We looked in the database and have called all the big companies, but there's no record so far of a Justin Mikkelson."

"So what has this boy done that people are after him?" She kept her eyes, as well as her question, directed toward Giff.

"He got a girl pregnant, and the family of the girl needs to talk to him."

"I don't know any Justin." She struggled to keep her voice level. "I don't think I can help." She clenched her teeth.

"Mr. Walker has a picture." He pointed toward Brent, whom

she was glad had not said anything. "We were thinking he might be going by an alias."

Out of the corner of her eye, she saw Brent's hand holding something. She glanced at it. She needed to get out of there. "I'll see what I can do." Which would likely be nothing.

"Thank you."

She nodded to Giff, then said to Brent without looking at him. "Mr. Walker." She stepped out of the office and the building without waiting for him. She paced by the curb. How could he do this to her? She'd had such a good time with him yesterday, but apparently it had all been a lie.

"Haley, I know you're upset with me but—"

She strode to her bike and yanked it free. " 'Haley, you're my north. You give me direction. I'm spinning out of control.' " She waved her hands in the air. "I can't believe I ate that up and let you use me."

"I didn't use you. I meant every word I said to you."

She turned toward him, and he halted. "Did you think I could lead you to this person you are looking for?"

"Yes, but—"

"Did you ask for my help, beyond asking if I knew the person?"

"No, but—"

"You used me! And what is worse is that you knew how I felt about people using me. You made it a point to ask me about my family."

"I never meant to use you."

"That's the trouble with users; it's who they are. They do it like instinct." She spun on her heels and marched her bike away.

He grabbed the seat of her bike on the opposite side from her, then gripped the handlebar.

She tried to jerk the bike free, but he held fast to it, so she let go and walked away from him as fast as she could. She heard her bike thump against the curb. She would come back for it later.

He jogged around in front of her and blocked her path. "Haley, stop and listen to me."

She stopped. "I wouldn't believe anything you told me now." This was too much for her to deal with right now.

"I can explain." He held out his arms.

"Don't bother. I can't believe I was so gullible. I feel like such a sap. I'm too old to be this naive again."

"You are not gullible or naive."

He had no idea. "You want to know why I left home? I'll tell you. My fiancé didn't see any reason to get rid of his girlfriend. And for a wedding present, she was getting an apartment. He was only marrying me to get in good with the boss, my dad, and to get a job promotion. I would have been married more than two months by now. A farce." Tears blurred her vision, but she blinked them away. She would not cry in front of him. "I believed him when he told me he loved me and he cared. He only cared about his job. He was using me. I thought I had learned my lesson, but then along comes a swarthy rogue PI and I get sucked in again. I'd say both *gullible* and *naive* fit." She moved around him and stepped off the curb almost in front of a pair of dapple gray horses.

The horses sidestepped her, nervously stomping and snorting, and the driver reined them to a stop. "Haley?"

"Jason. Wait right there." For once she was glad to see him.

As she walked past Brent, he reached out for her. "Haley, please."

She swung her arm out of his reach. She hefted her bike

onto the back of the flatbed dray that had a dozen or more cases of soda loaded on the front, then climbed on and scooted toward the front.

Jason said, "Isn't that the guy you were with yesterday?"

"Unfortunately, yes."

Brent came toward her. "Haley, can we at least talk about this?"

"Go, Jason."

Jason put the team into motion. She saw Brent watching her ride away. The tears she had held at bay broke free. She covered her face with her hands. When would she learn?

After a bit, the dray came to a stop. Jason climbed over the seat and sat next to her. He wrapped an arm around her and pulled her to him. She let him. She knew she shouldn't but did and cried into his shirt. She knew any progress Shane had made last night on getting Jason to understand where he stood with her would be lost in this moment. She pulled herself together and backed out of his embrace.

"Are you all right? He didn't hurt you, did he?"

Not in the way he meant. "No. He lied to me. Shouldn't you be with the horses?"

"Leave it to you to be worried about animals when you are so upset. I have the reins." Jason reached for her face with his free hand and leaned toward her.

As much as she wanted comfort right now, she took his hand and moved it away. "Jason, don't."

"Why not? It's no secret I have feelings for you. You're upset, and I want to help."

"It wouldn't be fair to you. I can't return your affections."

"If you gave us a chance, maybe you would."

"I can't." She climbed down off the dray and turned to him.

"Thank you for everything."

Jason didn't reply but looked at her with what appeared to be longing and suffering.

They were on a narrow utility road that was rarely used. She unloaded her bike and pedaled away. *Lord, please help Jason understand.* She had only made matters worse with him in her desperation to get away from Brent.

A half mile away, she stopped. Where was she going? She only wanted to be alone. She headed for her dorm room.

She opened the door to her room and cringed. The lump in her roommate's bed told her Gwen wasn't up yet. Gwen had worked a late taxi shift, then stayed out with friends until Haley had fallen asleep after two. Now she wished she had opted for a single room above one of the shops as Veronique had. But when she had come to Mackinac, she hadn't wanted to be alone. She wanted the activity of others in the hallway. Not today. She tiptoed back out.

She pulled her bike from the rack. Where could she go now that she wouldn't risk running into Brent?

Oh no! Shane! He was planning on meeting her and Brent for lunch. That wasn't happening.

She pedaled as fast as she could and walked into the Victorian Tea Shoppe. "Is Veronique here?"

Mrs. Oaks stood behind the counter. "In the back. She's getting her purse before she goes to lunch."

"Thanks."

Veronique met her before she reached there. "*Cheri*, I was just going to see you. Shane invited me to meet your Lone Ranger. I hope you don't mind."

Normally she would be glad, but right now she didn't want any of her friends to be subjected to Brent. "Could you tell

Shane not to meet me? Tell him I'm not having lunch with Brent after all, and I'll talk to him later about it."

"Is everything all right? You seem upset. Shane said you had a nice day with Brent yesterday."

"No. I am. I did. But then there was today. And Jason. Just tell Shane not to go to the Yankee Rebel."

Veronique pulled a key out of her purse. "You wait in my room, and I'll be right back."

"Thanks, but I need to be alone right now. I'll see you at dinner."

"I'm meeting Shane down the street. You come tell him. Zen we three can eat lunch someplace."

She wasn't up for lunch or talking to anyone about this yet. "No, thanks." She grasped Veronique's arm. "Just don't eat at the Yankee Rebel."

"No. Not without you."

"Thanks for doing this for me."

⁂

Brent sat across the street from the Yankee Rebel until three in the afternoon. Haley never showed up—not that he expected her to, but he had hoped. Hoped desperately for a chance to explain himself. To tell her it was a big mistake. To make it up to her. To hold her again. But none of that seemed likely at the moment.

Brent strolled around town without purpose. He leaned against a building across from the carriage tour company. Haley sat aboard the carriage waiting out front. How could things go so wrong with her in such a short time? Yes, he had been secretive, playing at being a private eye, but she had blown it all out of proportion. Why did it have to be such a big deal to her? So he was looking for someone. That didn't make what they had any less real.

Haley checked for traffic, looking back down the street. Her gaze skimmed his side of the street. His first inclination was to duck and hide, but he didn't, and she didn't seem to see him. She pulled out, and he watched her until her carriage was out of sight. Then he walked to the ferry and boarded the next one departing.

Once back at Dalton's, he stretched out on the couch and tucked his hands behind his head. *What do I do now, Lord? Do I give up searching for the Mikkelson kid? Would that win Haley back? Or do I fulfill my promise to Mr. Jackson and Kristeen?*

He recalled the look on Kristeen's face when she had sneaked out the back door and met him by his truck and the anguish in her voice when she asked him to tell Justin she was sorry. Sorry for what, she hadn't said. But he could tell she cared a great deal for the boy, and she seemed like a sweet kid. The two of them had obviously let their relationship go too far. Now Mr. Jackson was trying to fix the problem for his daughter by ensuring that nothing went wrong in placing the baby for adoption.

He got up and changed into his running clothes and took off out the door. Was there any way to do it all? Find Justin, help Kristeen, and win Haley back? Maybe once he found Justin on his own, Haley would be less upset with him. Maybe all she needed was a good night's sleep to calm her down; then he could talk to her rationally.

He could tell Mr. Jackson he was unable to locate the boy and return the money he had received. Mr. Jackson would send someone else. Would that be so bad? *Lord, is that my out?* He sensed a distinct *No. I don't want this job anymore. I know I asked You to give me a case right away, but this is more than I bargained for.*

After his run, he showered and dressed and was about to grab a soda from the refrigerator when Dalton walked in the front door. "I didn't expect you back from the island until the last ferry."

"Things went badly with Haley today."

"How bad?"

"She won't talk to me. I might have seen the Mikkelson boy today, and I don't even care."

Dalton whistled. "What happened? Yesterday was so perfect."

"I decided to get help in finding the boy. I went to the local police on Mackinac Island. The officer there brought in a carriage driver to show me around, help me with some leads."

"Haley?"

He nodded. "She took all our time together as my using her to find the boy. Yes, to be honest, I thought she might lead me to him, but I hardly even thought of him when I was with her. Now I'm stuck between finding Justin and getting Haley back. The two seem contrary to each other. I feel I have to choose between them, and I don't want to because I know what the choice would have to be."

"The boy?"

"I made a promise to Mr. Jackson. I made a point of telling him I was a Christian and he could trust me. If I back out now, not only could it reflect poorly on the Lord, but I don't think that is what the Lord wants. I believe He wants *me* to find Justin."

"Then trust that the Lord will work things out with Haley."

"What if He doesn't want me with Haley?"

"Then this misunderstanding would have happened later over something else. Isn't it better for it to happen sooner, as opposed to later when your heart is more invested in the relationship?"

"Would you still have dated and married Joslin if you had known you wouldn't have her that long?"

"You know I would. It was meant to be. All I'm trying to say is that if it is meant to be, you'll work things out with her, and if it's not, it's better for it to end before you both get too involved."

"But you said she was my type and you could hear wedding bells."

"The truth is, I think you two are meant to be together. You're like a perfect fit."

He hoped so. He wanted Haley at his side. Maybe always.

"Fight for her, man. She's worth it."

"How do I do that and still find the boy?"

"When I first proposed to Joslin, she turned me down and then broke up with me. But I couldn't give up. She said she didn't know me. 'Show me your heart,' she kept saying to me. Show Haley your heart."

"How do I do that?"

"Tell her what's in your heart."

"I did that last night, and she threw it back in my face this morning."

"Tell her your hopes and dreams. Tell her you totally messed up and are sorry."

"I don't know if *totally* messed up is quite accurate."

"Tell her you didn't understand before, but you do now, and you'll try not to make that mistake again. And if none of that works, pull out Matthew chapter eighteen, verse twenty-two, about forgiving seventy times seven."

"Isn't that a bit low, forcing someone to forgive you?"

"A desperate man in love will do things he never thought he would, when the relationship with the woman he loves is on the line. And it's not forcing her to forgive you but reminding her of what Jesus commanded. Then it's up to her to follow it or not. You're just pointing her to what is right."

"You used that on Joslin?"

"No. She used it on me. I had a falling out with her dad shortly after we were married. She pointed out my error in not forgiving him. 'If we do not forgive one another, how can the heavenly Father forgive us?' You don't want Haley living with her unforgiveness, do you?"

"And Haley thinks I can put a spin on things. That sounds a lot like manipulation for my own gain. I think I'll just let the Lord work on her for now. If she doesn't come around, maybe, just maybe, I'll point out a few Bible verses she might want to consider."

❧

Haley left the barn after her last run. She had come to her senses and remembered she was expected back at work. She had been tempted to call Big John and tell him she didn't feel well, which was true, because the whole situation had made her ill. She was thankful Brent had not reappeared. It hurt so much that he would lie to her and use her. He was supposed to be different. She rode to the church and knelt before the Lord in one of the pews. But what to pray? *I hurt, Lord.* She could think of nothing else, so she just stayed there.

After a while—she didn't know how long—she stood and went out to her bike. She should go and eat, even though she didn't feel like it. The others might be waiting for her.

Once at the dining hall, she took her food tray and searched for a table. She choked at the sight of her friend. It was the same face in the picture Brent had been holding. She wanted to cry.

eleven

Shane drank the last of his chocolate milk, then glanced up and saw her. "I was about to send out a search party for you."

Haley put her food tray on the table and sat down. "Where's Veronique?" She didn't want to talk about herself or why she hadn't been there earlier.

"She had to eat early and get back to the shop. I barely got here before she left. I thought Jason would have been here, but I haven't seen him."

A small blessing on a lousy day. One less thing to deal with at the moment.

Shane went on. "We talked last night. He seemed to understand."

After her encounter with him this morning, he was probably more confused than ever. But she couldn't tell Shane about that without telling him about Brent and why he was on the island—and that she knew Shane's secret. He was the last person she would have guessed to get a girl pregnant out of wedlock—and then leave her.

"Veronique asked me to tell you to come by the shop at closing time so the two of you could talk. What happened with lunch? Veronique said it was canceled. She also said you seemed upset."

"It didn't work out. You didn't go there, did you?"

"I thought about it." He shook his head.

"But you didn't go?"

Shane pinched his eyebrows together. "No. Why?"

She focused on her tray and picked up her fork. "I wouldn't have wanted you to waste your time." Brent would have recognized Shane as being Justin, and then Shane would have been trapped. This way she could talk to Shane without involving Brent. And if Shane wanted to leave the island without talking to Brent, she wouldn't stop him. She pushed around her spaghetti and meatballs on her plate.

"It's best while it's still hot."

If she ate it, her stomach might reject it at this point. "You want to go?" She couldn't talk to Shane here.

"You hardly ate anything."

She took a swallow of milk. "I'm not hungry."

"You're not?" Shane eyed her plate like a starving orphan in a third world country.

She traded plates with him. "Dig in." Someone might as well enjoy it.

It took him all of five minutes to scrape it clean.

She drank the last of her milk. "You were a hungry boy this evening."

"I hate to see food wasted." He stacked her tray and dishes with his.

"You ready to leave now?" She pushed away from the table.

"Let's go." He carried their trays over to the dish depository, and they left the dining hall.

Shane shoved his hands into his pockets. "You want to talk about it?"

Did she? She would rather pretend today never happened, but she couldn't do that. Pretending wouldn't change anything. Brent still would have used her, and Shane still would be Justin. Then she said the first thing that popped into her head.

"I was going to be married the first weekend in June."

"Whoa. A little change in subject there? I thought this was about Brent."

Brent. Kennith. It was all the same. Betrayal was betrayal. Brent had unknowingly reopened the wound Kennith had inflicted. "I don't want to talk about Brent right now."

Shane shook his head. "But you do want to talk about not getting married?"

"It's what brought me to this place in my life."

Shane shrugged. "Okay. So what happened with your wedding?"

"Kennith had a girlfriend he wasn't planning to get rid of."

"Ouch."

"I went to his office to surprise him, but I was the one surprised instead."

Shane turned toward her. "He was there with her?"

"No. His office was empty. I sat in his high-backed leather desk chair—that I bought him to help support his bad lower back—and turned it away from the door. He was supposed to come in and turn his chair around to sit in it and have a wonderful surprise of me there to take him out to lunch." They arrived at her dorm, and she sat on the curb outside.

Shane joined her, draping his hands over his bent knees. "He never came?"

The night was cooling off, so she pulled her sweater closer around her. "Oh, he came, but he wasn't alone. I could hear a professional-sounding female voice. Then once the door shut, it was less than professional. She was complaining about how much time he spent with *me* and how after we were married she would never see him. He told her he would rent them a special apartment and that he was only marrying me to get the promotion. That he loved only her and marrying me was something he had to do. The worst part is that he had the gall to hire her as his assistant. How cliché is that?"

"I can see why you left him." Shane picked up a twig from the ground and twisted it in his fingers. "Did you ever reveal yourself?"

"You bet. I couldn't resist. I wasn't about to let him lie his way out of it or try to explain it away."

"What did he say?"

"Not much. I spun around in the chair, not that either of them noticed. They were a bit occupied with each other. I cleared my throat, and they jumped apart. Then I asked, as if it were no more important than a shopping list, 'Is this the other woman?' "

"Busted." Shane chuckled. "I would have loved to have seen that."

"I introduced myself as the ex-fiancée, gave her my ring, and walked out."

"You should have kept the ring." He tossed the stick across the street.

"I didn't want anything from him."

"Did your dad fire him?"

"I don't know, and I don't care."

"You just left?"

She nodded. "I packed a suitcase, told my sister to tell the rest of the family the wedding was off, and walked out the front door."

"You were still living with your parents?"

She waited for a horse-drawn taxi to pass so she wouldn't have to compete with the traces jingling and the clomping of the hooves before continuing. "Off and on. Mom and

Grandma talked me into moving back into the house before the wedding. It would make planning easier. If I'd still had my apartment, I probably wouldn't have come here."

"So he was left to explain everything to your family."

She shook her head. "If I know Kennith, he probably played the innocent victim. I can hear him telling my parents, 'I had no idea she was unhappy. She never told me the wedding was off. Probably cold feet. I'll give her all the time she needs.' He would always put a spin on things to make himself look good."

She knew someone else who could make things spin his way. She didn't want to think about Brent. The pain went too deep.

She shouldn't put it off any longer. She wanted to know about this girl Brent was accusing Shane of getting pregnant. But how could she bring it up without revealing she already knew about the girl? And then that would lead to Brent, and she didn't want to discuss him now. But then again, she could tell Shane that Brent was looking for him and see what he wanted to do.

Shane was so grounded. How could he have ended up in this kind of mess? The girl, changing his name, running away. She wasn't so naive to think a Christian never got into that kind of situation, but Shane would have owned up to his responsibility. He wouldn't have run away. He wasn't like her. She looked at Shane, then back at the ground.

Shane raised his eyebrows. "Was there something else?"

"No." She couldn't ask. It was none of her business. She sat in silence wondering what Shane was thinking. Did he think about the girl? Did he even know?

"I left someone behind, too." Shane picked up a small rock and hurled it sideways across the street. "I guess you could say I was running away."

Did he want to talk about his situation, too? So it was all true. He'd run away from his responsibility.

"There was a girl—her name's Kristeen." He smiled when he said her name. "I was in love with her. Still am."

She squeezed her eyes shut for a moment. She hadn't wanted to believe he got a girl pregnant, then left her, but here he was telling her about it.

"She became involved with a twenty-five-year-old man. She was only sixteen. The creep was married, too. He got her pregnant." He picked up another twig and tossed it into the street.

Shane wasn't the father. She gave a mental sigh of relief. So why did Brent think he was? "What happened?"

"She was afraid he would get in trouble and told her dad I was the father of her baby."

"Why would you go along with that?"

"It's what Kristeen wanted." He found another rock and rolled it around in his hand. "He could have gone to jail because she was a minor. Kristeen begged me to go along with it. Her dad told me never to see her again. So I left town and came here. I would have done anything for her. I still would."

"What about you and Kristeen?"

"She never saw me as anything but her best friend." He hurled the rock harder than the last one.

"Doesn't it bother you that she's using you?"

"It's what I wanted to do. Besides, if I hadn't helped her, I wouldn't have come here. If I stay until the end of the season in mid-October and get the bonus, I might be able to start college after Christmas instead of next fall."

"Finding the good in a bad situation?"

"I guess. God uses both the good and the bad in His plans."

Was there any good in the situation with Brent? She couldn't think of any. She took a deep breath and asked again, "So it really doesn't bother you that she's using you?"

He shrugged. "If you want to use the term *used*. I prefer to think of it as helping a friend."

She shook her head. "I hate being used—by anyone."

"It depends on how you look at it."

"Used is used. Anyway you look at it, it's wrong."

"But God uses us all the time."

"Now see—that is the one area I have a hard time with. I know God knows what He is doing, but I hate being a puppet."

"I consider it an honor to be used by God. You were using me. You needed to talk, and I was here to listen. We use each other as friends so we're not alone. Using people doesn't have to be a bad thing. The Lord says to fellowship together with believers, so we use each other to fulfill that command."

"That's not the same. It's not using if it's mutually beneficial. When someone uses you, even God, you have no control."

"Of course you have control. You can choose to let God use you for His good."

"What about people using you?"

"Try not to look at them as a burden but as an opportunity for God to use you to touch their lives."

"That's a nice way to look at it, but I don't think I can do that." She was tired of people using and manipulating her. Maybe if more time had passed since Kennith's betrayal, she wouldn't still feel so wounded. Brent had come along at the wrong time. Was that God's plan, so she wouldn't fall for another Mr. Wrong?

Shane tapped the knee of her jeans. "It's about closing time.

I'll walk you to the tea shop. If I don't, Veronique will scold me in French."

She looked at her watch. "Have we been out here that long?" She stood and stretched the stiffness out of her legs.

Shane nodded and walked her to the shop where Veronique worked. "You want me to hang around?"

"No, go back to your room. I might be late."

"Give me a call when you're ready to go. I'll come over and walk you to your dorm." He started to leave, then turned back. "Haley, I hope things work out with Brent. If you want me to talk to him for you, I will."

"No," she said too quickly, then tried to recover. "I have to work things out on my own, but thanks for offering."

He nodded and walked away.

Veronique locked up, and Haley followed her upstairs to her room above the shop. Haley sat at the foot of the bed and pulled her feet up under her.

Veronique sat at the head of the bed and stretched out her legs. "Tell me what happened today."

"It's been a horrible day." She told Veronique about encountering Brent at the police station, what happened with Jason, and learning of Shane's innocence.

"So zat is why you didn't have lunch. What did Shane say about zis?"

"I haven't told him, and you can't tell him either, not about Brent or what happened with Jason." Shane was innocent and didn't need to be bothered by any of this.

Veronique frowned in disapproval. "Shane is your friend. He would want to know. Should he not know zat a private investigator is looking for him? He could tell him he is not zee father, and zat would be zat."

"If Shane's not the father, why bother telling him at all? He doesn't need to be upset by this."

"Why bother telling him? It is his problem. No? He should have zee opportunity to deal with it or not. Shane is an adult, is he not?"

"I wish I wasn't involved."

"Maybe zee Lord put you between Shane and Brent so you could help Shane."

That sounded a lot like God using her again. "What if I don't want to be in the middle?"

"I think you are too late for zat." Veronique folded her hands in her lap.

"What if I refuse to let God use me?"

"Zen Shane will be all by himself. And won't Brent eventually find him?"

She let out a heavy sigh. "Probably. You are making this hard for me. It was easy when I was angry at Brent and protecting Shane. I don't want to do this."

"Why do you not want God to use you?"

"I don't want to feel like someone else's puppet."

"Zen don't be."

Finally someone was on her side.

"Choose to do what zee Lord wishes you to do. Zen you have no strings."

Would she be happy as a puppet without strings? And would she be happy obeying the Lord's prompting?

"Zee sooner Brent and Shane meet, zee sooner Brent will leave and you can get over him."

Was that possible? The ache for Brent was stronger than she had felt for Kennith. "I wish I could make the hurting stop."

"He was in your heart. You cannot make him leave. Zee

hurting will stop when he leaves your heart on his own or someone else comes and pushes him out." She moved her hands forward as if she were pushing an invisible person.

"I'm not looking for someone else for a very long time."

Veronique pulled her knees up to her chest. "You were looking for Brent?"

"No."

"Zen it could happen when you are not looking, like with Brent. Or maybe you will make up with him."

"I don't know that I could trust him again. What kind of relationship would that be?"

"Not good. But maybe you could trust him again."

Trust was hard to rebuild once broken. The pieces never fit back the same. There were always gaps and ridges.

It was one in the morning when Haley left Veronique's. She felt a damp chill in the air. She didn't live that far away and didn't want to bother Shane. More than that, she didn't know what to say to him yet. She should tell him about Brent but didn't know how. Once she reached her room, she picked up the phone and dialed Shane.

"Haley?" His voice sounded as if she had awakened him.

"Yes. Sorry to wake you."

"I was waiting for your call. I'll be right over."

"Don't worry about it. I'm already back in my room."

"You didn't wait for me?"

"I got home safe. That's all that counts."

"I guess so. Thanks for calling." He yawned. "See ya."

"Bye."

If Veronique was right about her heart, she hoped she could control it. First Kennith and now Brent. She couldn't trust herself to make a good decision where men were concerned. Shane was a good kid, but had she misjudged him, as well? Was he guilty of what Brent said he was and simply didn't want to admit it? Maybe if she told Brent that Shane was not the father, he would be satisfied with that and she wouldn't have to bring Shane into this.

twelve

Brent flipped up the collar of his navy fleece jacket to keep the mist off his neck and stepped up to the ticket window. Would Haley even let him board her carriage? "One, please."

The girl behind the window took his money and, as she was passing the ticket across the counter to him, smiled. "You're back. I think that will make Haley happy."

He wished he could be so sure of it. He nodded and took his ticket. "Thank you."

The plastic sides of the carriage that had been rolled up to the roof the other days were hanging down to protect the passengers from the moist air. He took a seat at the back of her carriage. Haley didn't refuse to let him board, but her look told him she was none too happy with his presence. Her hair hung in two thick braids, one on each side of her head. She looked cute like that.

At Surrey Hills, he disembarked with the other passengers and started the line to board again. Haley stared at him but didn't move her carriage forward. He could wait her out, and he sensed she knew that, because she clicked the horses into motion. She stopped by him but kept her gaze forward.

He climbed into the front seat behind her. "So what are the names of these horses? Are they Thor and Thunder?"

Her shoulders rose as she took a deep breath. "Let's not even pretend small talk is appropriate."

Maybe small talk wasn't appropriate. But if he could get her to talk to him, he knew he could fix this. "Have lunch with me, please."

"I don't date fudgies."

The flatness to her voice squeezed his heart. "I want to explain."

She held up her hand. "Don't bother. I know who it is you are looking for."

That news should make him happy, but it didn't. "Haley, you don't have to do this. I'll find him on my own." So he had been right that she knew him.

"You don't need to bother. He's not the father of that girl's baby."

"How do you know?"

"He told me." Her back was stiff and straight like a soldier under inspection.

"And you believe an eighteen-year-old kid?"

"Definitely. He's a good kid." She was trying to protect him.

He scrubbed his face with his hand, allowing his whiskers to dig into his palm. "Let's say you're right. I'll still need to talk to him. So it doesn't change anything."

She spun around in her seat and looked at him for the first time. "Why would you need to do that? Don't you believe me?"

Proceed with caution, Brent. You've never been on such thin ice before. "Of course I believe you. But how would it look if I went back to the girl's father and told him someone who knows the boy told me he's not the father? But if I talk to Justin myself and hear his side of the story, then I can tell Mr. Jackson I'm sure Justin is not the father." Of course he wasn't sure at this point, but he hoped that was the conclusion he would reach after talking to the boy. He desperately wanted Haley to be right, but he knew an eighteen-year-old was more than capable of lying to keep himself out of hot water.

"I won't turn in my friend."

"I thought you didn't know any Justins." He saw moisture gather in her eyes.

She faced forward in her seat. "I didn't know that was his name."

He was itching to ask her who he was and what name he was going by, but he was determined not to do or say anything to make her think he could be using her. "When I find him, I'll tell him you didn't give him up." A family of five boarded the carriage. He was going to let the conversation die for now, but Haley continued.

"Let me talk to him first."

Why? Did she want to warn Justin? Or was she saying she was willing to help him? "You don't have to do that." He didn't want her help if it put him in deeper trouble with her.

"I think it would be better for him to hear it from me that you are looking for him than for you to show up at his work site or dorm room."

Did she realize she'd narrowed the field for him? "If that's the way you want it. When?"

"Tomorrow."

"Why not today?"

"I probably won't see him until dinner."

He wanted to get this over with, so he could focus on fixing things with Haley. "So then, why couldn't I see him after dinner?"

"Tomorrow," she said more firmly.

What was she up to? Probably nothing. "Fine. Tomorrow it is."

&

After Brent stepped down, Haley wanted to cry. Had she

made a deal with the enemy on behalf of her friend? She let herself be distracted by the passengers boarding for her next tour. She had work to do and would focus on that. After work, she would decide how to proceed.

When her shift was over, she pulled up the hood of her rain slicker and pedaled to the Little Stone Church and sat in a pew. She liked this quaint old building. It wasn't large, but the solid structure of stone on stone gave her a sense of stability and strength.

She didn't pray. She knew in her heart what God would tell her to do.

An older couple came in and looked around. They took pictures of the large stained-glass windows that showed some of Mackinac Island's history.

Haley studied the windows, as well, from her seat. The detail in the pictures was incredible; the history came to life. The fudgies left, and she was alone again.

As she gazed at Father Marquette, a missionary to the local Indians, a verse from Jeremiah came to mind. *"Before I formed you in the womb I knew you, before you were born I set you apart; I appointed you as a prophet to the nations."* Certainly Father Marquette had been known and set apart for God's work. Her gaze shifted to the Indians, and they, too, were set apart.

She closed her eyes. *And I was set apart.* "Before birth, Lord?" She knew the answer. Yes, even before she was born. How the Lord could know her and know she would ask Him into her heart, she couldn't quite grasp, but she knew He could. "Have You set me apart for this? For Shane?" She had the impression the Lord was waiting for her to choose whether or not to do this task set before her. *"I consider it an honor to be used by God."*

Shane. He would want her to let God use her to help resolve this situation.

"Choose to do what zee Lord wishes you to do. Zen you have no strings."

No strings. Her choice. She swallowed and was a bit afraid to speak the words but did. "Use me, Lord." A peace washed over her.

❧

Haley sat against the wall outside the door of Shane's dorm room. It was better for her to explain things gently to Shane than to have Brent jump out of the bushes at him.

Shane came down the hall. "There you are." His hooded sweat jacket looked soaked through. It must have started raining again since she had been waiting. He swiped the hood off his head.

She pushed up against the wall and stood. "Can we talk?"

"Sure. But the rain's really coming down out there." He grabbed the sides of the centered front pocket and shook water off his jacket. "You want to come in to talk?"

"Thanks."

He opened the door and stepped inside. "Well, maybe that's not such a good idea. There's not much room in here." His room was about twice as wide as the twin bed shoved against the wall and about one and a half times as long. And it was chilly.

She smiled. "You always said you were living in a closet. And you really are."

"I kind of like it. I didn't want a roommate, and this is all that was left. But I have everything I need: a bed, a dresser with a lamp that looks like it might have survived World War II, a nice little window, and a closet rod."

The hexagon window above the dresser was hinged on one side and swung in about an inch, the reason for the cool temperature. The covers were pulled up on the bed, but she wouldn't exactly call it made. And the closet rod was just that, a rod angled across the corner of the room adjacent to the door at the end of the bed, and on it hung a jacket and another sweatshirt.

"You can leave that open," he said, pointing to the door. "Have a seat." He motioned toward the bed. It was the only place to sit besides the floor.

"This is fine." She sank down against the open door.

Shane pulled his wet sweatshirt over his head and tossed it in the bottom of his closet, then put a long-sleeved T-shirt over the one that had to be wet from the rain. After closing the window, he sat on the floor and leaned against the bed. He draped his arms over his bent knees. "What's going on, Haley? I caught up with Jason today; he said you broke things off with Brent and that you and he were getting close." He shrugged. "With Jason, that could mean a lot of things. He'll read something into nothing where you're concerned."

"That's not exactly the way it happened." *Where to start?* "I was upset with Brent and still am—but that's beside the point— and Jason came along. . . ." Actually Brent was the point in all of this. "It just got complicated."

She didn't want to do this. *Lord, can I change my mind?*

thirteen

"So something did happen between you and Jason?" Shane's mouth hung open slightly.

Haley leaned her head back against the door and stared at her friend. How did she explain what happened without confessing why she was so upset with Brent and revealing she had already known Shane's secret? Maybe if she started at the beginning. But which beginning? "Yesterday Giff needed some help at the police station, and Harry volunteered me. When I arrived, Brent was there."

"Was Brent arrested for something?"

She could see the concern for her on his face. "No. Why he was there is another issue. As I said, this is complicated. There are a lot of different parts, and they all collide and make a mess." She pressed her fingers together to represent the different parts and then had them bounce off each other to show the collision. "Does that make sense?"

"Not really."

She waved her hand in the air. "It doesn't matter. I'll explain what happened with Jason. I was surprised to see Brent and was mad at him—I'll explain that in a minute." She told him how she'd been outside the station when Jason drove by and how she'd hopped on his fray. She told about her crying and Jason holding her and everything she said to him. "I was upset and not thinking."

"Leave it to Jason to take that as something significant

happening between the two of you. He probably figured if you were on the skids with Brent, then he had an opening."

"I can't even pretend to understand what he is thinking."

"When I see him, I'll see if I can help him understand."

"Thanks."

"So what happened with Brent? I thought something must have happened when you canceled lunch yesterday. You were all mushy and sweet on him the night before last."

"Remember our talk last night—about being used?" He nodded. "Brent used me. The only reason he is on the island is because he is looking for someone and was hoping I could lead him to that person."

"What's the big deal about helping find someone?"

"It's how I felt he did it—sneaky and deceitful. He's a private investigator."

Shane's expression faltered, and he paled slightly.

Though she knew the answer, she asked anyway. "Who is Justin Mikkelson?" Was it his real name, or was Shane Peters?

Shane tipped his head back until it was resting on the bed. "This is about Kristeen, isn't it?"

"After you and I talked last night, I told Brent today you weren't the father. But he still wants to talk to you."

"Why?" Shane stared at the ceiling.

"He's not convinced you're not the father."

Shane pulled his head up off the bed. "I would be if Kristeen would let me. I'd marry her and take care of her and her baby. Her father would never let that happen."

Now that sounded like the Shane she knew—taking on someone else's responsibility. "Why did you change your name?"

Shane raked his hands over his short blond hair and clasped

them behind his head for a moment. Then he released them and raised his head. "I thought it was a good idea?"

"You don't sound convinced of that. Why go by Shane Peters if you are really Justin Mikkelson?"

"As you said, it's complicated."

"You don't have to tell me if you don't want to."

"It's not that." He shook his head. "Do I start at the beginning and work up to your question or start with answering your question and work backward?"

She understood that dilemma. "It probably doesn't matter."

"Shane was my big brother and mentor. Not my real brother. You know—the Big Brother program. It was my aunt's idea when I was fourteen. That's when she took responsibility for me. Aunt Aimee's a little ditsy, but she always tries hard. I could finally be a regular kid."

"Why did your aunt finish raising you? Did your parents die?"

He picked at a thread on the hem of his jeans. "Mom's still alive and probably my dad, too. Aunt Aimee became my legal guardian because no one else wanted me."

She found that hard to believe.

"I should shoot back to the beginning to make sense of this." He shook his head. "That would take too long and bore you. The short version: I don't know who my dad is—his name's not on my birth certificate. My mom is in a mental hospital to keep her from trying to burn herself alive again. And Aunt Aimee stepped in after Mom burned down the apartment building we were living in."

Wow.

He stretched out his legs as much as he could before they hit the wall. "Mom had talked about her little sister, but I thought she was making it up—like an imaginary friend—until Aunt Aimee finally found us. Mom seemed to be normal with her sister there, but I knew she wasn't. You couldn't tell anything was wrong. I was hoping for someone to notice my mom wasn't right, not like other moms. The day after my aunt left, Mom held my face in her hands before I left for school and stared at me. She had tears in her eyes. That was the closest I ever came to seeing my mom cry. 'Just like him,' she whispered, then opened the door and said, 'Have a nice day,' as if everything was fine."

Shane pulled his knees to his chest and wrapped his arms around them. "I didn't want to leave her. I wanted to stay. I had this bad feeling in my gut. I got partway to school, then turned around and ran as fast as I could back home. When I opened the door, my mom stood in the middle of the room with flames all around her. I dragged her out, but she wanted to go back in. She wanted to die in that fire; she wanted to die because I was just like him." He wiped his eyes with the heels of his hands.

Haley blinked back tears. "Like who?"

"My dad, I guess."

She never would have guessed that was his life. He was such a great guy. "So where did Shane Peters come in?"

"Aunt Aimee's idea. She thought I needed a positive male role model in my life. He was great and helped get me on track. I was a mess after Mom was hospitalized. He moved away a year ago, but we still keep in touch. When I came here to the island, I didn't want to be me anymore. I wanted to be a normal person with a normal life for once. I wasn't just running away from Kristeen's dad but from myself."

"You are a neat guy exactly the way you are. You don't have

to change your name to be a better person. Whatever you call yourself, you are still the same wonderful person inside."

"I think that's what God has been trying to teach me this summer."

"Are you sure there's no way you can be the father of Kristeen's baby?"

"Positive. We were never anything more than friends."

"So what do you want to do? Do you want to meet with Brent? I can tell him to go away. We have three docks in town. I could tell him to take a long walk. And if you want to leave the island, then he can look all he wants. I think there's still a ferry leaving tonight."

He smiled at that and released his legs. "Then I can be on the lam, running from myself." He looked at her sideways with a sly grin. "Is there anywhere I can go where I won't be there also?"

"I guess not, but you still don't have to meet with Brent." She wanted to help Shane any way she could.

"I'll meet with him."

"Are you sure?"

He stretched his legs again. "No. But I don't see a good reason not to. And maybe he can tell me how Kristeen is doing."

"I want to be there with you, if you want me to be."

"I'd like that."

She smiled. "Okay. It's my turn to play big sister to you, but I can't miss any more work. Let's plan for our lunch break in the park."

"Are you going to meet him at the dock in the morning and tell him?"

She shook her head. "No, I have work."

"How will he know where to meet us?"

"He'll find me."

❧

Dalton came back into the house sweaty from his workout. "You look awful."

Brent was on the couch where he had sat, unmoved, for an hour. "Hey, thanks. I needed cheering up."

"You looked like a whipped puppy last night, and I thought you looked about as bad then as you could—but you've outdone yourself."

He leaned forward with his elbows on his knees and scrubbed his face with his hands. "I saw Haley today."

"Didn't go so well?" Dalton wiped his face with the towel around his neck.

"It went great. She knows who Justin is and is going to set up a meeting tomorrow. I feel like a heel." He looked up sideways at Dalton. "What do I do now?"

"What do you want to do?"

"I hate it when people answer your question with a question."

Dalton sat in the green recliner. "What do you expect when you ask a question that only you can answer?"

"And another question?"

Dalton threw up his hands. "Man, Haley's worth fighting for. Is it possible to find this boy without hurting her anymore?"

"I don't know."

"You could always take her in your arms and kiss her until she forgives you."

He rolled his eyes. "There's a winner of an idea. She'd probably slap me or worse—and never speak to me again."

Dalton shrugged. "I never said it was a *good* idea."

"Do you have any *good* ideas?"

Dalton leaned forward. "This boy's a friend of Haley's, right?"

"She said he was."

"Then you can either accept her help, thank her profusely, and treat the boy with the utmost respect—which you would do anyway—and therefore gain some of her trust back. Or you could thank her for her offer to help you, then go find the boy on your own, also gaining back some of her trust."

He stared at Dalton.

Dalton raised his eyebrows. "You have to admit those are decent ideas."

"They put me right back where I was when I asked, 'What do I do now?' "

"Okay, so what do you want to do?"

He laid his head on the back of the couch. "Give up."

"That wasn't one of the options I offered."

He leaned forward. "I want to be able to sit down with Haley and reason with her and fix this."

"Buddy, let me give you a little piece of advice. I know I'm not a font of wisdom, but I have learned a thing or two being married even for a short time. Women don't generally want us guys to fix anything—unless it's something like the garbage disposal or computer. When it comes to emotional things, it's best just to listen."

"If she won't talk to me, then I can't listen—and fix this."

Dalton shook his head and headed off to the shower.

He wanted to fix this. He needed to fix it. But he didn't know how. How could he convince Haley to listen? To understand? He had never felt this bad about Michelle or anyone else. The break with Haley hurt deeper than anything since his dad had died.

❧

Brent woke at three in the morning, pulled his laptop onto his stomach where he was lying on the couch, and switched it on. He flipped through Haley's file. His heart ached to relive the day they'd spent together there on the mainland. "What can I do to make it up to you, to help you understand?"

fourteen

The early morning service had not yet begun when Haley scanned the inside of the church and found Shane, Jason, and Veronique sitting in a middle pew.

Jason sat on the aisle. "We can all move down." He started to stand.

"That's okay. I can sit down there." She scooted past Jason and Shane and sat on the other side of Veronique.

Veronique leaned over to her. "Did you tell him?" She raised an eyebrow toward Shane, who was sitting next to her.

Haley nodded. "We're meeting Brent at noon." She leaned forward to look past Veronique and touched Shane's arm. "I'll meet you on Market Street in front of the post office. We'll walk over together from there."

Shane nodded. "Does he know to meet us there?"

"Not yet."

"How will you tell him?"

"He knows I drive a carriage. He'll come."

"You're sure."

"He wants to find you."

Shane looked a little pale with that comment. Haley knew he wanted to meet with Brent, but it was obvious he was also nervous about it. She hoped she was doing the right thing. But then it wasn't her decision; it was Shane's. She was only going to be there to support her friend.

❧

The day was cool and cloudy when Brent stepped off the ferry, but at least the rain from yesterday had stopped. He scanned the people milling around the dock but didn't see Haley. He had expected her to be at the dock—well, half expected. Had she changed her mind about helping him? He had changed his mind about accepting her help. He was going to do this on his own and show her he wasn't trying to use her.

He headed toward the carriage tour site and skimmed as many faces as he could while walking in case Haley was on her way to the dock. He didn't want to miss her. He stopped across the street from the carriage loading area and waited. The first carriage came and went. And the second. But the driver of the third was the familiar face that made his heart pick up its pace. She wore her hair in braids again. He'd forgotten her hair weapon. He should have brought it to return to her.

He stepped off the curb and nearly sideswiped a bicyclist. Fortunately the girl was coasting slowly, and he reached out to balance her. "I'm sorry. My fault."

The girl looked up at him, and her smile broadened. "No problem." She pedaled away but glanced back at him.

He took a deep breath and continued toward Haley's carriage, circling around the front of the horses. He put his hand on the front of the carriage. "I thought you'd be at the dock this morning."

She kept her gaze on the edge of the carriage. "I can't miss any more work."

"I hadn't thought of that."

"We'll be at the park at noon or so if you still want to talk to *Justin*."

She strained her voice a little on "Justin." "That won't be necessary. I'm going to find him on my own."

She looked at him for the first time. "For some strange reason, he wants to meet with you. So we will be there. Please don't waste his time."

He wanted to beg her to reconsider. If he could just talk to her so he could gauge how she felt about helping him; but her carriage was filling up, and this was no place to have that kind of discussion. "I'll be there. By the statue."

She checked for traffic, and he stepped back and watched her pull away.

So now what was he supposed to do? Look for Justin until noon and hope he found him first? Or do nothing and wait for noon?

∾

Near noon when she rode up the street toward the post office, Shane was sitting on the curb with his hands hanging over his knees, his bike parked near him. She stopped her bike in front of him but still straddled it. "Are you nervous?"

"My palms are sweaty." He stood and wiped them down his denim shorts.

"Just tell him the truth, and you'll be off the hook. You haven't done anything wrong. He can't make you do anything or go anywhere you don't want to."

"What if he's a cop and is here to arrest me?"

She swung her leg over the back of the bike and got off. "On what charge? Helping a friend? Lying? They don't put people in jail for that. And I don't think he's a cop." At least she hoped not. But she had been wrong about him before. She never would have guessed him to be a private investigator looking for her friend either.

❧

Seagulls dotted the grass in front of Brent as he stood by the statue in the middle of the park. Several contingents of tourists—fudgies, as Haley would call them—congregated for lunch. Would she come? She had said "we," but maybe only Justin would come. Should he have come? Was he doing the right thing? He could leave before they got here. No, he had said he would be here. He had to keep his word.

A blond kid about nineteen or so swaggered toward him and stood chest to chest with him. "Stay away from Haley."

"And who are you?"

"A friend. A *real* close friend."

The young man was implying they were more than friends, and from the look in his eyes, he was jealous. Was there something between him and Haley? He didn't want to believe so, but the boy's attitude told him Haley meant something to him. And Brent had trodden on his territory. Was this the boy from the wagon the other day? "Are you Jason?"

"What of it?"

"Just curious." He wasn't about to get into a scuffle, verbal or physical, with one of Haley's friends over nothing.

"Just stay away from her." Jason poked him in the chest.

Brent kept his hands deep inside his pockets. He wasn't sure how much to read into the boy's words or actions.

Seemingly satisfied, Jason turned and strutted away. Brent was glad that was over.

The sun broke through a small opening in the cloud-covered sky, and he looked up. *Lord, please let this meeting go well.* He gazed across the park and saw two people walking bikes across the grass, Haley and a teen—Justin.

His pulse picked up its beat at the sight of her, and he let out a long breath. *Lord, guard my tongue and help me say the right words.*

Haley introduced Brent, then presented Justin as Shane Peters.

He held out his hand. "It's nice to meet you—Shane." Haley had made a point to introduce him by his alias, so Brent would go with that for now.

Justin shook his outstretched hand. "It's Justin Mikkelson. Wow, it feels good to admit that."

Haley leaned against the base of the statue with her arms folded, watching him like a mother hen protecting her young.

Brent kept Haley in his peripheral vision. He wanted to focus on her and straighten out things between them, but this meeting was about Justin. "Thanks for meeting with me."

"Kristeen's baby isn't mine!" The words practically erupted from Justin, and he seemed to relax a little having said them.

He wanted to believe the boy, but he needed more than his word to take back to Mr. Jackson for this to be over for Justin. "But she claims it is."

"It can't be. We never—you know."

"Then why is she saying it is?"

Justin told him the story of the older man and how Kristeen was lying to protect him. Justin relaxed more as he talked.

Brent believed Justin, but convincing Mr. Jackson might be another story. "Do you know who the father is?"

Justin looked down at his feet. "I promised not to tell."

"I can respect that. I'll see what I can do to convince Mr. Jackson to search elsewhere." He glanced at Haley. Her flat expression never wavered.

"How is Kristeen doing?"

He turned back to Justin. "She's doing as well as can be expected. She's going to have her baby soon."

"This is all my fault. I talked her out of having an abortion."

"None of this is your fault. You were only trying to help her."

Haley pushed away from the statue and took hold of her bike to walk it. "Shane, we need to get back to work."

Justin looked at his watch. "Sorry, man—I gotta go."

"Can we talk again this evening? I'll buy you dinner." He noticed Haley wouldn't call him Justin.

"If you're buying, I'm there," Justin said.

He figured an eighteen-year-old boy could always use a free meal, and he appreciated his coming. "Tell me where to meet you."

Justin picked a restaurant and gave him directions.

Brent turned to Haley. "The invitation is for you, too."

"I'll pass."

He ached to reach out and hold her but knew she wouldn't let him. "May I see you after dinner?"

"I don't think so." She turned to leave.

Justin shrugged and grabbed his bike, then jogged to catch up with Haley. "All this talk about food is making me hungry. I'm starved."

Haley laughed as she and Justin were walking away. Brent followed in the same direction a few paces behind them to hear her reply.

"Come to the barn with me. I have a box lunch under my carriage seat. You can have it."

"Really?"

Brent stopped and let Haley walk away from him, but he could still hear her next reply. "I'm not going to eat it."

Brent smiled. But she had to eat sometime.

❧

Haley was waiting for her afternoon passengers to board when

Brent stepped up to her carriage. She hadn't expected to see him. He held up a bag and a cup. "I heard you give your lunch to Justin. I figured that was partly my fault, so I bought you a hamburger, fries, and a cola."

She had to admit he had been nice to Shane—or rather, Justin. And now he held up a peace offering. So why did she feel as if he were trying to buy her affections? "I appreciate the thought, but I'm not hungry. Also I can't eat while I'm driving."

He lowered the bag and cup, disappointed.

"I hate to see food go to waste. Shane—that is, Justin—is working maintenance around the island school. He could eat two or three lunches. That's where it will do the most good."

He simply nodded. "Where's the school?"

"Take Main Street until it turns into Lake Shore Boulevard. You'll be heading northwest. The school's on the right." She had to admit he was trying. But she couldn't go back to the way it was that one perfect day. Maybe the day had been too perfect. She wished he'd quit coming to her. She didn't want to keep rejecting him. She wanted to put this all behind her and move on with her life.

fifteen

Brent sat across the restaurant booth from Justin, waiting for their order to arrive. He wasn't sure why he'd asked to meet Justin tonight. He had all the information he needed; but the young man was his link to Haley, and he wanted to hold on to what slim thread he could.

Justin took a long drink of his soda and drained it down to only ice. "Hey, thanks again for the hamburger at lunch."

"Sorry it was a little cold. I bought it for Haley. She told me to take it to you."

"Oh, sorry. She can't eat while she's driving."

"That's what she said. I was hoping to make some headway with her. I think she would be happy if she never saw me again."

"I don't think so. She wouldn't be this upset if it didn't matter so much to her."

"Thanks. I never meant to hurt her." He leaned forward on the table. "You know her pretty well. How do I undo this?"

Justin shrugged. "Beats me." The waitress came with their food, and Justin turned toward his plate with round eyes. "If you figure out girls, let me know." He wrapped his mouth around the double-decker burger. He had already consumed an entire order of onion rings.

Brent thanked the waitress as he took his hamburger.

Justin wiped his mouth with his napkin. "Jason's always doing stupid stuff, and it doesn't seem to bother her at all. She likes you in a different way from how she likes Jason."

Different? Was different good? "So do you think she'll forgive me?" He bit into his burger. It was much better than the ones he'd cooked at Dalton's.

Justin picked up the ketchup bottle and shook some onto his plate. "I would like to say yes, but it's so hard to tell with girls. I had a friend in high school whose girlfriend broke up with him. She claimed she loved him and cried every time she saw him. I'll never figure that one out." He picked up a fry and dipped it into the ketchup. "Girls are weird when it comes to emotional stuff. They shouldn't work so hard to make it difficult." He popped the fry into his mouth.

So Justin didn't have any more insight into women than he did. If Justin, who knew Haley better than he did, couldn't help him and Dalton, who had been married, wasn't much help, then he was on his own to figure it out.

Except for the drone of the other patrons talking, they ate in relative silence until Justin finished his hamburger and was mopping up the last of his ketchup with his final fry. "I want to go back with you."

"That's not necessary." He left his remaining fries and pushed his plate aside.

"I want to see Kristeen. Could you get Mr. Jackson to let me see her?"

"Are you sure that's what you want to do? You could be done with this here and now. I believe you, and I'll convince Mr. Jackson you're not the father."

Justin nodded. "I want to see her."

"All right. I'll make it happen. Mr. Jackson wants your signature on a release form. We tell him you want to see Kristeen first—which is only right. If you're going to shine a light on her lie, it would be good for her to know first. After you've seen her, I can break the news to Mr. Jackson, if you'd like." He wished solving his problem with Haley would be so easy.

"Are you full?"

Justin shrugged. "Not really."

"Would you like to order another burger?"

"No. I'm fine."

That meant, *I'm still starved and could probably eat this table, but I won't.* Brent remembered what it was like to have a metabolism that worked faster than he could eat. "If you're still hungry, I don't mind buying you more food."

"You've already done enough, but thanks."

He wouldn't push it. The waitress came then with refills of their drinks. "May I have the bill?"

"Sure." She took their empty plates away.

Brent turned back to Justin. "Do you think Haley will talk to me again?"

Justin was taking a drink through his straw but stopped and swallowed. "I wish I could tell. I never would have guessed she'd get this upset about such a little thing. It's not like you're Kennith—oops."

He could take a wild guess as to who Kennith was. "Her ex-fiancé with the girlfriend?"

Justin's eyes rounded. "She told you about that?"

"Sort of. She was kind of yelling at the time."

Justin nodded. "I can understand her running away from him. But something like you looking for me? I wouldn't have guessed that would have made her so mad."

"I don't think it was that I was looking for you; it was that she didn't know about it."

"I don't see what difference that makes. I can try talking to her for you."

"I'd appreciate that." The bill came, and he nodded an acknowledgment to the waitress.

"You're really crazy about her."

"Yeah, I guess I am."

"I know how you feel. I'm that way with Kristeen."

"May I pray with you?"

Justin's eyes widened in what looked like both surprise and gratitude. "Sure."

Brent prayed for Justin, for Haley, and for himself, that the Lord would work out His will in all their situations. Then he put enough money down on the table to cover the bill and tip. "You ready to go?"

Justin stood. "You don't have to catch a ferry yet?"

He looked at his watch as they headed for the exit. "The last one's not for a while."

"Why don't you hang out at the park? I'll get Haley to go over there." Justin smiled mischievously.

"I don't think that would be too good. You won't try to force her to see me, will you?"

"I'll strongly encourage—and maybe throw in a little guilt. I'm sure deep down she wants to talk to you."

"Justin, that's not fair."

Justin smiled and winked. "All's fair in love and war. And I think this might be both. You're going to help me see Kristeen. I'm returning the favor. Just be in the park." He jogged off before Brent could protest any further. Not that he wanted to.

❧

"He's at the park."

Haley glared at Shane, who was standing outside her door.

"Well, that's nice for him. I'm not going."

He smiled.

What was that smile for? She narrowed her eyes. "What?"

"You'll go."

She folded her arms. "No, I won't." And she wouldn't let him talk her into it.

"You will."

She was more stubborn than he. "What makes you so sure?"

"Because he's waiting for you."

"*Grr.* You are so infuriating."

He held out his elbow like an old-fashioned beau. "I'll walk you over."

"Well, if you're going to the park, you might as well tell him I'm not coming."

"If you don't go, then neither will I, so he'll still be waiting for you."

She balled her hands and stomped her foot. "You are impossible."

He had the gall to smile—again. "Shall we go? We don't want to keep Brent waiting."

Haley yanked her jacket off the end of her bed. "I may never speak to you again for this."

"Sure you will."

She turned and glared at him. "Don't be so sure."

"But I am, because I'll be waiting for you to talk to me again."

She threw up her hands. "I give up." She headed out the door, knowing he would be right behind.

Now more than ever, she didn't want to see Brent. He was manipulating her by waiting, knowing she would come. Manipulation was akin to using. She didn't like either. Well, she would give him a piece of her mind before she left him standing there.

Shane took her arm to stop her before she entered the park. "Haley, one more thing. I told him to wait in the park. He didn't want to do it. Didn't want to force you to see him."

"Shane!"

He smiled and turned to go. "He made you happy."

She watched her friend walk away and was unsure what to say to Brent now. She closed her eyes and took a deep breath to calm herself, then marched toward him where he was leaning against the statue.

Brent stepped forward. "You came." He sounded relieved.

"Only because of a little manipulation."

He held up his hands. "It wasn't my idea."

"He told me, but that doesn't make me like it any better."

Brent motioned toward a bench. "Would you like to sit down, or are you planning to leave?"

"I'll stand."

"Does that mean you're going to leave?"

"I don't know. Maybe."

"Then I'll talk fast."

"No, I'll talk. Shane said he was leaving with you." She still couldn't think of him as Justin. "Promise me you'll have him come back right away. If he takes only a few days for a family emergency, he can return to his job and still get the bonus." He had told her he was leaving just before he told her Brent was waiting for her in the park.

His eyebrows pulled slightly. "I can't make that promise. I have no more control over Justin than I do you. I can try, but I can't force him. I promise I'll come back."

"That's not the promise I want. I want him to go to college, as he's been dreaming of doing."

"I'll do everything I can to make that happen."

She searched his eyes to see if that were true.

Then he said, "I'm sorry my actions looked as if I was using you. I never set out to do that."

"Why couldn't you tell me from the start you were an investigator looking for Shane?"

"I should have, but Kristeen's father wanted everything hush-hush. I can't change that now. But you have to believe me that I never meant to hurt you."

She sighed. "I don't know what to believe anymore."

He held out his hands. "I'll do whatever I can to make this up to you."

"I let my guard down here." She fisted her hands. "I felt safe. This place is so perfect. I didn't think anything could hurt me here."

"I'm sorry. Please give me a chance to prove it to you."

She shook her head slowly. "I don't know how to trust you, how to trust myself." She fought to hold back the moisture in her eyes. "Maybe nothing between us was real. I thought it was real with Kennith and was wrong."

He grabbed her shoulders. "I'm not Kennith. I'm nothing like him."

The earnestness in his gaze tugged at her. "I have to go." She twisted out of his grasp and turned away from him.

"Haley," he said, then more insistently, "Haley."

She picked up her pace, but he snagged her arm and pulled her to him and kissed her.

She pushed away and kept her gaze down. "Brent, I can't do this right now." She struggled against the tears. "Please let me go."

He put his finger under her chin to raise her head. "I'm afraid if I let you go, I'll lose you."

She met his gaze. "You can't lose what you don't have."

"Please don't say that."

"I have to go." She turned and walked away as a tear rolled down her cheek.

⁂

The next evening, Haley stood off to the side with Veronique as Shane and Brent unloaded Shane's luggage from the horse-drawn taxi. She just couldn't think of him as Justin. He would always be Shane to her.

He walked over to her. "Brent bought me a ticket."

"I can't believe you are leaving."

"Kristeen needs me. I'd still do anything for her."

"But you are coming back?"

"I don't know yet." He rubbed his short blond hair with his hand. "If staying will be more help to Kristeen, then I'll stay."

"What about college?"

"I'll get a job there." He looked over toward Brent standing by the ferry ramp. "Go over and say something to him."

She glanced at Brent, then back at Shane. "We said what we needed to last night."

"Haley."

Tears filled her eyes. "You'd better go. The ferry will be leaving."

He sighed and walked to the boat.

Veronique stepped up beside her. "You're not going to say good-bye to him?"

"It's best if I don't."

Veronique was quiet for a moment. "Good."

She turned to her friend. "Good?"

"Zen zair is no end, and he is welcome to come back."

"That's not the reason."

"No matter. It still works."

She watched the ferry start to motor backward away from the dock. "What if this whole thing with Brent was a rebound from Kennith? What if the Lord was saving me from another bad relationship?"

"And what if you are afraid and are using zis to protect yourself?" Veronique put a comforting arm around her shoulders.

"I don't know if I'm willing to risk it. I've always played it safe and taken chances on the things I could win."

"You can never tell if you will win in love until zee end when you are gray and wrinkled. Only God can you be sure of."

She stood silently beside her friend as the ferry slowly maneuvered away from the dock. Brent leaned against the railing and raised his hand to her in a wave. She lifted her hand in reply and left it there until the ferry was out of sight.

"When your heart heals, you will want him to come back."

"Maybe it's best this way. No false hopes."

"And maybe you will wish you had said a proper good-bye and given *him* some hope to come back for."

"You are a hopeless romantic."

"*Oui.*"

❧

Haley pulled up her carriage to receive her first afternoon group of fudgies. Summer was coming to a close, and a lot of the seasonal help had left already or would be leaving soon. It had been nearly a week since Shane had left with Brent. Jason had started his freshman year at Western Michigan, and Veronique would head back to France next week. That would be a teary good-bye.

Her carriage filled, and the last passenger to step aboard in the back was Dalton, a pair of headphones hung around the collar of his royal blue golf shirt. She smiled at him, and he smiled and waved back. Another Lone Ranger.

At Surrey Hills, Dalton got off and went inside the gift shop like all the other passengers. She thought he would have at least said hi. But then he could be mad at her for not making up with his friend. It wasn't that she didn't want to; she didn't know how to trust him again. She pulled forward to wait for the departing passengers.

Soon Dalton appeared beside the carriage. "May I climb up?"

"Of course."

"I've been debating whether or not to give this to you." He pulled a gold CD in a blank jewel case from his pocket. He handed it to her. "I burned a song for you. Brent wouldn't like me poking my nose in this matter. He's too nice to tell you that you are only hurting yourself by not forgiving him." He gave her a lopsided smile. "But I'm not so nice."

She stretched out her hand to give it back to him. "Thanks, Dalton, but I don't have any way to play this. I didn't bring a CD player."

He quickly pulled off his headphones and handed her the CD player out of his pocket. "Here—take this."

"I can't take your CD player."

"It's no big deal. I have another one at home."

She reluctantly took it and tucked it all beside her seat. "Thank you." Her carriage filled with tourists, and it was time to leave.

Once back in town, the passengers disembarked. "It was good to see you, Dalton," Haley told him.

"Same here." He backed away and gave her a little wave.

She wondered the rest of the day what song Dalton had burned for her. After she unhitched her carriage and finished up with her other duties, she took out the CD as she walked to her bike. She saw no song title written on it—only two Bible verses from Matthew. She wasn't sure she was ready to listen to the one song Dalton felt she needed to hear. She tucked it in her jacket pocket and rode down to meet Veronique for dinner.

sixteen

Haley looked out the window of her dorm room. September was winding to a close, and the trees were clothed in the radiance of brilliant fall colors. Red, yellow, and orange leaves dotted the streets and lawns.

All her friends had left, and the Bible study dispersed. Even her roommate was gone. It was lonely, especially on her day off.

She pulled out the CD she had been avoiding for a month and sat on her bed. She opened the player and saw it already had a CD in it. Dalton probably didn't realize he had left one in his player and had likely been wondering what had happened to it. She would return it to him with the player when she left the island in a couple of weeks. She reached for the CD he had made for her but stopped. She still wasn't ready to listen to it.

She felt justified in her anger and was afraid that whatever Dalton had chosen could change her. She had been avoiding the book of Matthew because she knew that scripture could change her more than anything else.

She listened to the CD he had left in his CD player instead. Interesting how it was the one with the song "The Wonderful Cross" she had picked out for the three of them to play. She closed her eyes and played along on an imaginary piano. The words touched her as they never had before. She had not laid this burden down at the foot of the cross. Though she had let God use her, she hadn't forgiven Brent.

Once again, the Lord had used music to open her heart to listen to Him.

She put in Dalton's CD and listened to it. The song he'd chosen was "Forgiveness." The message: forgive before it was too late.

Lord, I don't want to forgive. He hurt me, and I want to hold on to the anger.

She pulled her Bible off the nightstand and opened to Matthew, chapter eighteen, verses twenty-one and twenty-two, the first of the two references Dalton had written on the CD. "Then Peter came to Jesus and asked, 'Lord, how many times shall I forgive my brother when he sins against me? Up to seven times?' Jesus answered, 'I tell you, not seven times, but seventy-seven times.'"

"How can I forgive seventy-seven times or even seven times when I can't forgive once?"

One at a time.

She turned back to her Bible. The second reference was chapter six, verses fourteen and fifteen. "For if you forgive men when they sin against you, your heavenly Father will also forgive you. But if you do not forgive men their sins, your Father will not forgive your sins." The words were in red. Jesus was speaking directly to her. *How do I forgive when it hurts so bad? I don't know how. Please show me.*

The image of Jesus hanging on the cross battered and beaten came to her mind. *"Father, forgive them, for they do not know what they are doing."*

Was it that simple? Just say it? She took a deep breath. *I forgive Brent.* She felt lighter, but it wasn't enough, so she spoke it aloud and gave it conviction. "Brent, I forgive you. And, Lord, forgive me for my stubbornness not to forgive." A peace swept over her and washed away the hurt and anger.

She took the sarong Brent had bought her at the Mystery Spot out of her bottom drawer and wrapped it around her shoulders. *Forgive me, Brent.*

❧

The next evening, the phone rang. Justin's familiar voice greeted her. "I wanted to let you know how things turned out here."

"I have been dying to know." Haley sat on the floor under the phone on the wall.

"Kristeen had her baby, a girl."

"Did she decide to keep it?"

"No. Her dad made her adopt it out. I wanted to adopt little Lacy, but Brent and Aunt Aimee talked me out of it."

Brent and Justin's aunt together sent a wave of sadness through her. Had he found her more receptive to his affections? She took a deep breath and returned her focus to Justin. "Why would you want to adopt someone else's baby when you're only eighteen?"

"I figured Kristeen would want to see her baby one day."

"And you'd be there waiting for her."

"Silly, huh?"

She pulled her feet up under her. "I think it's sweet. But I'm glad you're not going to be the baby's adoptive father."

"I think I am, too. Brent has helped me see that Kristeen is not the right relationship. He says going to college will be good for me."

Thank you, Brent. Was it only last night she had finally forgiven Brent and let the whole matter go? And for the first time, she could think of Shane by his real name, Justin. "Will you have to put off college until next year? Or do you think you can find a job for the next couple of months that will make up what you would have earned if you'd stayed here? I could even give you some money to help out."

"No need to. I'm already enrolled at Western Michigan. I'm rooming with Jason. He has a girlfriend, and she's really good for him."

"You're at college? How is that possible?"

"Brent found me a four-year scholarship—tuition, books, housing, the whole works."

"Brent found you a four-year, full-ride scholarship just as school was starting?" That didn't sound plausible.

"He knows a man who likes to do that sort of thing anonymously for worthy students. Brent told him about my situation, and he did it. He set up an account that he'll transfer funds into each term."

It sounded a little fishy to her. What was Brent up to?

"Aunt Aimee is glad. She always felt bad that she didn't make enough money to send me to college. We barely scraped by."

Aunt Aimee—that was what Brent was up to. She would guess that *Aunt Aimee* was young and pretty. And she had probably caught Brent's eye. "I'm glad everything is going well for you."

"Haley, you can't tell Brent I called and told you this."

It wasn't as if she would ever get to talk to him again. "What does it matter?"

"He wants to tell you everything."

"Why?"

"He thinks it will force you to talk to him because you'll want to know. You'll talk to him, won't you? You're not still sore at him?"

"What about your aunt?"

"Aunt Aimee?"

"Oh, never mind. Of course I'll talk to Brent. He can call me anytime."

"He's not here. I'm at college. He stayed to help with some last details. He also wanted to make sure Kristeen will be okay through all this. I asked him to tell me how she's doing."

"Do you have a number where I can reach him?"

"If I told you that, then he would know I talked to you. He's coming to the island when he's finished. To see you."

To see me? "In two weeks, the Grand Hotel closes and the season is over."

"He knows that."

So maybe there wasn't anything between Brent and Justin's aunt after all. But just because he was coming here was no reason to get her hopes up.

"What if everything is different? What if we don't have the same easy camaraderie?"

"What if you do?"

"Things have changed for both of us."

"Haley, promise me you'll give him a chance."

"Is that what he said—he wants a chance?"

"Well, no. Only that he promised to come back."

So there it was. Brent was only coming back to fulfill a self-imposed obligation. She would put no hope in a relationship blooming again.

seventeen

The last passengers of the last tour of the season thanked her and stepped down onto the sidewalk. She glanced around one final time but saw no smiling Brent aiming his camera at her. He hadn't come after all. She clicked her tongue and snapped the reins. "Let's go home, boys."

Haley knew better than to put any kind of hope in a promise made out of guilt. It had obviously been nothing but an empty promise to smooth over her ruffled feathers. But she had wanted him to be different, had hoped. Why hadn't she sat down and talked with him? She had probably pushed him away. She couldn't blame him for not coming back. He probably thought she was too high maintenance. Justin had said he knew when the season was over. Brent had to know she would leave after that. He had chosen not to come.

She had no way to contact him. She hadn't even remembered to get Justin's phone number at college. Before she headed home, she would stop by Western and visit Justin and Jason, but she wouldn't ask Justin for Brent's phone number again. If Brent didn't want her contacting him, she wouldn't push it. She would write Brent a letter, and when she returned Dalton's CD player and CD, she'd ask him to give it to Brent for her.

She gazed at the Grand on her left. Would she be back next year? She would have to see how things went with her family. She couldn't—wouldn't—stay with them forever.

Ahead on the right, she glimpsed movement. A man in a brown leather jacket stood by a tree and hiked up one black pant leg to his knee, exposing a hairy shin and calf. He stuck out his thumb.

A smile pulled at her mouth. *Brent!* Always the flirt. She would not get her hopes up though. She would wait and see what he said.

She pulled Thor and Thunder to a halt. "I have a policy never to pick up hitchhikers."

He leaned on the side of the carriage. "Then why'd you stop?"

"You were scaring my horses."

"Was I?"

She nodded. "You'd better climb aboard so they can't see you." Before she finished her sentence, he was seated behind her.

He tugged his pant leg down and held up a bag. "I bought some fudge. I guess that makes me an official fudgie."

"I guess it does." Now that he was here, she wasn't sure what to think. She was a little nervous. What if his feelings for her had waned?

"Oh, and I have this for you."

A gift? That was a positive sign. She turned to receive it. The hair clip he'd taken from her when they'd played miniature golf. Her heart sank as she accepted it, and tears sprang to her eyes. First, the fudge was an obvious barrier, like "*See—I'm off limits.*" And her hair clip had been a tie between them, albeit a small one, and he'd just severed that.

She was getting uncomfortable and wanted a topic that wouldn't lead to disappointment. "I talked to Justin a couple of weeks ago."

"You did?" Now he sounded disappointed.

"You gave him a full-ride scholarship?"

"He wasn't supposed to tell you about that. He doesn't know it's me."

"He still doesn't, as far as I could tell. Why did you do it?"

"I couldn't bring him back here, so I thought the next best thing was to send him to college. Did he tell you about Kristeen, as well?"

She nodded and maneuvered the horses into the barn. "You can wait over there if you like, while I take care of the horses." He jumped down and stood off to the side. When she was finished, she got her bike and joined him. She sat on the seat of her bike and walked it with her feet.

Brent walked beside her. "Where to now?"

"I didn't have any special plans. I was going to pack before tomorrow."

He jammed his hands into his jacket pockets, and the bag of fudge crinkled. "So today is your last day?"

"Yes." She had hoped by saying she had no plans that he would want to make plans together. "Tomorrow it's back to the real world."

"Where are you going from here?"

She smiled and thought of Justin telling her she would go back home, even before she knew.

He swung his gaze her way. "Why are you smiling?"

"I was just thinking of Justin. He knew before I did that I would go home."

"To your family you ran away from?" He sounded surprised.

"It's the only one I have."

"You aren't going back to your ex-fiancé, are you?"

"No way." She hadn't even thought about him, but she supposed it was likely she would see him. "Maybe he's left and I won't have to see either him or her. Is that too much to hope for?"

"We can always hope. Without hope, we would be—hopeless." He rubbed his hands together and blew on them. "It's a lot colder here than I thought it would be."

"The air has a definite biting chill in it today. They're talking of snow tonight and tomorrow."

He pulled his hands inside his coat sleeves, then reached for the handlebars. "Let me take that." She let go but didn't have a chance to get off before he grasped the handles, then stepped over the slanted center bar and put his foot on the lower pedal.

"What are you doing?"

"Getting us into town faster."

"By riding double?"

He twisted around. "Sure. Haven't you ever ridden double on a bike before?"

"Not since I was a kid."

"Well, hold on."

"Your hands will freeze." She tugged at her leather work gloves. "Here—wear these."

"I doubt they'll fit."

"They're a little big on me. It's worth a try. Better than frozen fingers."

He had to pull hard to squeeze his hands into her gloves, but he managed. "Mmm. Nice and warm." He gripped the handlebar and glanced over his shoulder. "You ready?"

She tucked her hands inside her heavy coat sleeves and placed them on his waist. "I can't believe you're doing this."

He stood on one pedal and hopped on his other foot. "If I can get us going, I'll be doing this."

She giggled. "You want me to drive?"

"I think I have it." He pushed with his free foot as though he were riding a scooter and started them rolling.

She pushed, too, with her dangling feet.

He tried several times to lift his foot to the upper pedal before he finally succeeded; then he pumped standing up. "Piece of cake." He swerved trying to keep their balance.

"Whoa." She held on a little tighter.

"I have it—we're okay."

They sped up. Haley held her feet out from the bike. "Wheee!"

"Which way?" he asked at an intersection.

She pointed. "That way." Then she pointed out her building, and Brent stopped in front of it. She put her bike in the rack.

Brent returned her gloves. "Thanks."

"I should thank you." She slipped her gloves on. *Toasty warm.* "That was fun."

Brent was quiet as he walked her toward the door. What was he thinking? Why had he come back? What if he was here out of some sense of duty? She hoped it was more but wanted to know instead of second-guessing. "Why did you come back here?"

He put his hands inside his jacket pockets. "I promised you I would."

Duty.

"I would have come sooner, but things with Kristeen's parents and Justin took more time than I'd anticipated. Then, with Justin going to school, it was that much longer. Don't you want me here?"

"I don't want you to feel as if you have to be here."

"Look, Haley. I know we didn't get off to the best start, but I really like you."

Yes! That was all she needed to hear.

"I also know I'm on thin ice with you. I don't want to push, but I want to be around you—as much as you will let me."

She smiled. "I came to grips with my flailing emotions and forgave you. Besides, what went wrong between us had more to do with my not dealing with the whole bad situation with Kennith. So the ice isn't so thin."

"Really?" She could hear the smile in his voice. "Is it thick enough for this?" He slipped his arm around her waist.

"Um-hmm."

"What about this?" He stepped in front of her to stop her and linked his hands at the small of her back.

She bit her bottom lip and nodded. "Do you want to kiss me, Brent?"

"Very much."

She twisted away from him and began walking again with a big grin. *Thank You, Lord, for bringing him back to me.*

"Hey, wait a minute. You can't ask a question like that and just walk away."

"Looks as if I already did."

He stopped her and turned her toward him. "Haley Tindale, I can't figure you out." He squinted his eyes and studied her. "I don't know if you asked that question because you're fishing for a kiss or because you just wanted to know where I stand."

She supposed she was fishing for both. "You won't know if you don't ask."

His mouth pulled up on one side. "I think I already know the answer." He put his hands on her waist. "Do you want me to kiss you?"

She bit her bottom lip again and nodded.

"Okay." He stepped away from her and continued walking.

"I just wanted to know."

She trotted to catch up. "You're not going to kiss me?"

He shook his head.

She stared at him. "You're really not?"

"Nope."

"Really? Then what are you going to do with that information?"

"Save it for later." Brent opened the dorm door for her and leaned on the edge of it. "I'm going to get a room and stay on the island tonight. Will you have dinner with me?"

"Depends on where." It really didn't matter. He could take her to a hot dog stand, and she'd go.

"How does the Grand Hotel dining room sound?"

Like the perfect ending to a wonderful summer. "You would need a coat and tie at the Grand."

He unzipped the front of his leather coat to reveal a silly cartoon tie and a suit jacket. "And you a dress. I'd like to see you in a dress."

"What if I don't have one?"

He studied her a moment. "I'm guessing you do. But I'll ask anyway. Do you have appropriate attire for the Grand Hotel?"

"Blue or purple floral?"

"Blue or purple what?"

"Dress. Which one should I wear?"

He smiled, and her heart did a happy little dance. "Surprise me."

She dug a pen from her coat pocket but couldn't find a scrap of paper to go with it, so she took hold of Brent's hand and wrote her phone number on it. She signed her name with a large loop on the Y and put a smiley face in it.

He turned up his hand to see what she'd written. "A girl hasn't written on my hand since I was seventeen."

Good. She stepped inside. "I'll call the Grand Hotel dining room to make reservations and request a taxi to pick us up and take us there. You get your room and give me a call so I'll know where to come and get you."

"Shouldn't I be making all the arrangements?"

"I have contacts."

He continued to lean on the door and stare at her. "You are almost too cute to resist."

He would kiss her now. She was sure of it.

"I'll let you go and give you a call when I have a room." Brent released the door and turned to leave.

He really wasn't going to kiss her. She had expected him to grab her and pull her back and kiss her. But instead the door closed. She stared at it, then opened it. Brent was walking away. "Brent."

He turned with a satisfied smile on his face.

She ran to him, threw her arms around his neck, and kissed him. His arms came around her, and he held her tight.

He kissed her for a long moment before he pulled back, but he kept his arms around her. "Now you've done it."

"What?"

"I may never let you go."

She laid her head on his chest. "And I may never let you go."

He kissed her cheek and whispered in her ear. "I love you, Haley."

And she knew she was falling in love with him.

A Letter To Our Readers

Dear Reader:

In order that we might better contribute to your reading enjoyment, we would appreciate your taking a few minutes to respond to the following questions. We welcome your comments and read each form and letter we receive. When completed, please return to the following:

Fiction Editor
Heartsong Presents
PO Box 721
Uhrichsville, Ohio 44683

1. Did you enjoy reading *The Island* by Mary Davis?
   ❏ Very much! I would like to see more books by this author!
   ❏ Moderately. I would have enjoyed it more if

   _____

   _____

   _____

2. Are you a member of **Heartsong Presents**? ❏ Yes ❏ No
   If no, where did you purchase this book? _____

   _____

3. How would you rate, on a scale from 1 (poor) to 5 (superior), the cover design? _____

4. On a scale from 1 (poor) to 10 (superior), please rate the following elements.

   _____ Heroine   _____ Plot
   _____ Hero   _____ Inspirational theme
   _____ Setting   _____ Secondary characters

5. These characters were special because _____
_____
_____

6. How has this book inspired your life? _____
_____
_____

7. What settings would you like to see covered in future
   Heartsong Presents books? _____
_____
_____

8. What are some inspirational themes you would like to see
   treated in future books? _____
_____
_____

9. Would you be interested in reading other **Heartsong
   Presents** titles? ☐ Yes ☐ No

10. Please check your age range:
    ☐ Under 18   ☐ 18-24
    ☐ 25-34   ☐ 35-45
    ☐ 46-55   ☐ Over 55

Name _____
Occupation _____
Address _____
City, State, Zip _____